Jack & Sandy

One war. Two friends. Three generations.

A graphic novel by

Bob Kerr

Hi, I'm Jack Tait. I'd like to tell you about an adventure I had with my mate Eddie.

This is my dad, Alec. He dropped us off at the start and picked us up at the end and made sure we had all the right gear. He does worry a bit though.

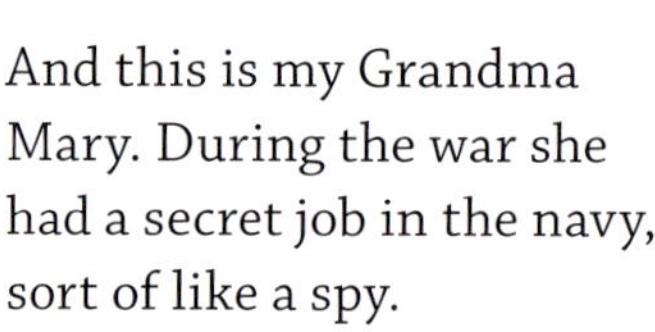

And this is my Grandma Mary. During the war she had a secret job in the navy, sort of like a spy.

This is my Grandad Sandy. After the war he disappeared. Eddie and I set out to find him.

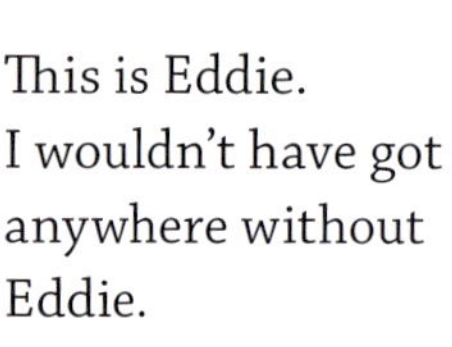

This is Eddie. I wouldn't have got anywhere without Eddie.

And this is my grandad's mate Billy. I never met Billy, but you could say he changed my life.

Not how it was supposed to start

Jack and Eddie, the Waihou River, 2001

MY DAD WAS A SHIP'S ENGINEER, I'M AN ENGINEER, AND YOU'LL BE ONE.

GRANDAD'S A BIT OF A MYSTERY. HOW OLD WERE YOU WHEN HE LEFT?

FOURTEEN.

I WISH I'D MET HIM.

WHY DID HE LEAVE?

Jack's dad pushed them out. 'Don't get swept under the willows,' he called as they disappeared around the first bend.

They were both surprised at the speed of the current. 'We'll be in Auckland by lunchtime,' said Eddie.

'Dad packed us enough food for a week,' Jack called back. 'He reckons it'll take us at least a week to get there.'

The sun flickered through the willows and the river stretched ahead of them all the way to the sea. They planned to paddle down the Waihou River and then up the coast to the Waitematā Harbour and right into Auckland.

There was a flash of turquoise and gold as a kingfisher darted across the river. Red matted willow roots slid past beneath Jack's kayak. Eddie pulled alongside.

'So, did you phone your grandad?'

'Yeah, well, sort of,' said Jack.

'How did you know where he was?'

'Found him in a suitcase,' said Jack, 'on top of the wardrobe.'

'What did he say when you opened the suitcase?'

'"Gidday, we've got to talk," — nah, the suitcase had his old camera and a photo album and a seaman's record book that listed all the ships

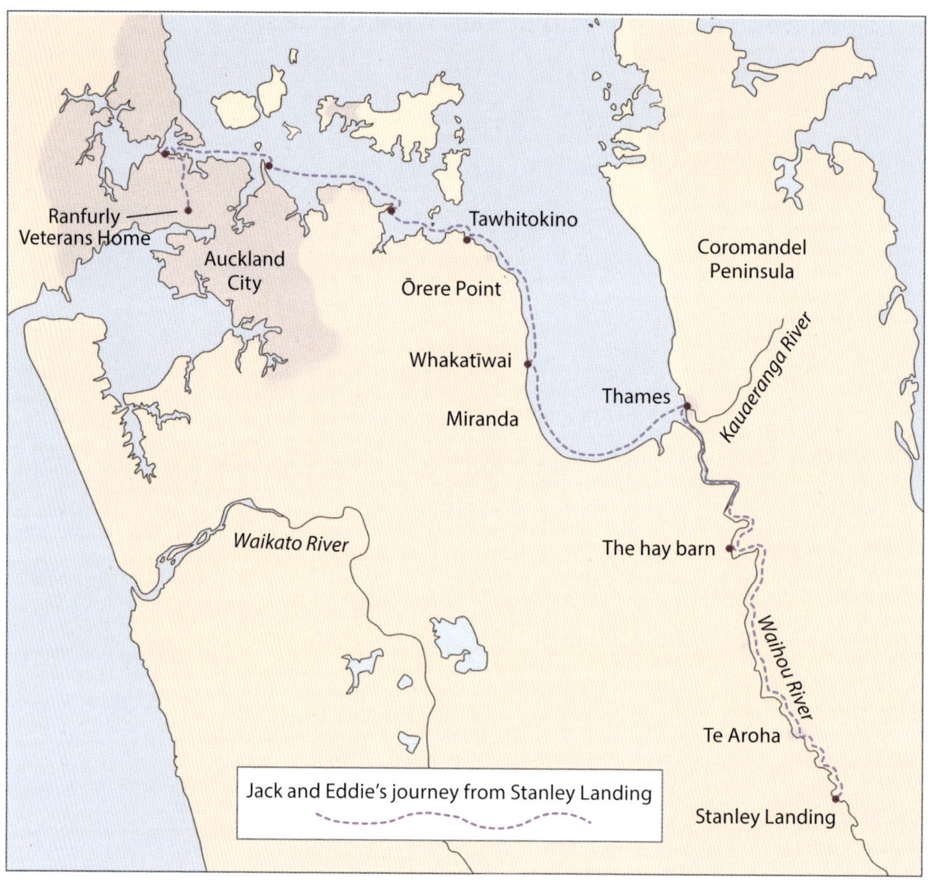

he sailed on — I've got it here.' Jack pointed over his shoulder at the back hatch. 'When Gran started losing her memory, she stuck yellow Post-it notes everywhere. Lists of things to do, names of things, there was one on the fridge that said fridge and one on the microwave that said microwave — that was after she started keeping the frozen peas in the microwave. There was this Post-it note on his photograph album that said "Ranfurly Veterans Home".'

'Did you tell your dad?'

'No, I phoned the Ranfurly Veterans Home and asked to speak to Sandy Tait.'

A swirl in the current slowly spun Jack's kayak around until he was facing the wrong way. Jack looked over his shoulder and carried on paddling backwards.

'The receptionist asked who I was, and I said, "I'm his grandson." She sounded surprised and said, "I didn't know he had any family," and went to find him.'

'Good work, Sherlock,' said Eddie. 'What did he say?'

Jack dug in his paddle and turned the kayak so that it was facing forward.

'He wouldn't take the call.'

'Not so good.'

'No.'

'So he doesn't know we're coming?'

'No.'

'And we're not a hundred per cent sure that he is your grandad.'

'No.'

'And your dad doesn't know that we're on the case?'

'No, he gave up trying to find him. I figured we shouldn't get his hopes up. Dad tried to keep track of him. He'd go to the library and spend hours reading through the electoral rolls until he found him, but the letters he sent were never answered. He'd go all silent and moody when there was no reply.'

'So we just rock on up to the Ranfurly Veterans Home and ask him why he buggered off?'

'Yeah, a surprise attack. I reckon if Dad could, I dunno, talk to him or something, find out why he left, he'd lighten up a bit, not worry so much.'

'How old would he be now?'

'Must be in his late eighties I reckon.'

'Hope he doesn't croak before we get there.'

They drifted along in silence, watching swallows darting after insects in the still morning air.

'And did you phone your auntie?'

'Yeah,' said Eddie, 'we can stay with her. The backdoor key is under the pot with the geraniums.'

In the middle of the river, a willow branch juddered back and forth in the current. Eddie went to the left. Jack followed, then changed his mind and backpaddled. The current swept his kayak up against the branch. He paddled forward. The kayak wouldn't move. He paddled backwards. The kayak wouldn't move. The current kept it pinned against the branch. Slowly the kayak began to

topple sideways. Jack grabbed at the branch, but his hands slipped off the slimy wood. The kayak flipped right over. This was not how it was supposed to start. Ten minutes into the trip and he was upside down. He fumbled for the front of the spray-skirt, yanked it off and found he couldn't wriggle out. He was running out of air. Bend forward, push from the back, he remembered. Out he popped. Gasping.

Eddie helped him pull the kayak onto the bank. They took the front and back hatches off and checked their gear — it was still dry. They each picked up an end, turned the kayak over and emptied the water out of the cockpit.

'I'm not getting back in that bloody thing,' said Jack. He sat down on the grass. 'Why didn't we take the bus?'

Eddie lay back on the grass and waited.

Jack looked up and down the river then reached for his wet lifejacket and put it back on.

'You should have seen the look on your face as you tipped,' said Eddie, passing Jack his paddle.

From Stanley Landing, Jack's dad drove down the river to the Armadale Road bridge. Last chance if they've forgotten something, he thought. He waited in the middle of the bridge. Where were they? Had something gone wrong? He looked at his watch. They should be here by now.

In the distance the two kayaks came out of the willows. He waved. The boys waved their paddles.

'You're wet,' he called, 'what happened?'

'We stopped for a swim', said Eddie. 'See you in Auckland.'

'Remember the weather is supposed to change this afternoon,' he called as they disappeared under the bridge. He watched them paddle away down the long reach on the other side. He could hear them laughing.

Around the next bend Eddie stopped paddling.

'It stops,' he said.

'What stops?' said Jack.

'The river, it stops.'

He pointed with his paddle.

There were willows on the left bank, willows on the right bank, and there in front of them also a wall of willows.

'Weird,' said Jack.

'Very,' agreed Eddie.

A tree had fallen from one bank to the other. Branches had been pushed up against it by the current, along with a jumble of driftwood and fence posts and a wooden farm gate. The current was sweeping underneath the logjam. This time Jack was cautious. He didn't get too close.

'We can't get through that,' said Eddie.

'Over there,' said Jack, pointing. He paddled back against the current towards the bank, grabbed a clump of weeds, swung his feet out into the mud, sank halfway up to his knees and scrambled up the bank.

Eddie swung out into the middle of the river and paddled hard for the bank. His kayak squelched up onto the mud, and Jack grabbed the front and gave it a pull. Eddie stepped out onto the grass with his feet still dry.

'You'll get your turn,' said Jack. They pulled the kayaks up through flax and blackberry, pushing willow branches out of the way as they went. They dragged them along the fence line until they found a place to slide them back down the bank into the water.

The river meandered its way across the flat farmland. On one bend a black swan came blundering out of the trees like a flying boat struggling to gain height.

As Jack looped around the next bend, two startled ducks came squawking out of the willows. They paddled frantically for the middle of the stream followed by one tiny chick.

'It's okay,' said Jack. 'It's not the duck-shooting season — I'm not after you for dinner.'

He turned the kayak to shepherd the parents back to their offspring, but the two ducks just paddled faster, squawking frantically at their young one to get a move on.

Have it your way, he thought and turned the kayak into the gap between the parents and the chick. When he was exactly between the two the seagull circling above dived. Screeching with delight, it snatched up the tiny grey ball of feathers and flew off.

Jack dropped his paddle across the cockpit and held up his hands in disbelief.

'You bastard!' he shouted after the disappearing gull. He turned and looked at the two silent parents in the middle of the river. 'I'm sorry, I didn't mean . . .'

'So who's a bastard?' asked Eddie when Jack caught up with him.

'No, not you,' Jack explained.

In the early afternoon, just past the bridge at Te Aroha, they ran the kayaks up on a concrete boat ramp.

'I could go a feed,' said Eddie.

As they walked back to their kayaks licking tomato sauce off their fingers, the first drops of rain hit the concrete. Back in their kayaks, they found the southerly breeze had swung around to the north, bringing showers that turned to steady rain. It swept in grey drifts along the stopbanks and left a pattern of spreading circles on the river. It was difficult to tell exactly where they were. The only markers were the bridges at Tirohia and then a few hours later the highway bridge north of Paeroa.

From the stopbank five cows watched them. One of them raised its tail and squirted out a jet of brown lumpy liquid.

'So remind me why we're here,' said Eddie, as the rain beat on his parka hood, 'and is it safe to drink the water?'

'Perhaps not,' said Jack.

'There is one other problem,' said Eddie.

'What's that?'

'We're going backwards.'

Jack looked at the cows up on the stopbank. Despite paddling towards them, they were no closer. 'The incoming tide must come this far up the river,' he called to Eddie.

They pushed on into the wind and the rain. On the other side of the stopbank they could hear the sounds of a busy road and see the tops of huge trucks going past.

'That must be the highway to Auckland,' said Jack, looking at the map. 'We should be coming to the Cook Memorial.'

Eddie pointed towards a small wooden jetty. They climbed out and walked to the top of the stopbank. A stream of traffic, windscreen wipers slapping back and forth, raced past, sending up showers of spray. A picnic table sat next to a block of white painted concrete with the words 'Cook Memorial' on it.

'What's this Cook Memorial?' said Eddie.

'Captain Cook, 1769, he rowed up here in the *Endeavour*'s longboat. It was all tall kahikatea forest then. Dad told me about it.'

'He knows stuff, your dad, drops us off, picks us up, makes sure we've got the right gear.'

'It's called worrying,' said Jack.

Eddie pulled up the cuff of his parka and looked at his watch. 'Not much daylight left.' He pointed across the highway to a hay barn tucked into a row of gum trees.

'I reckon,' said Eddie. They walked back to the jetty, pulled the kayaks up the bank and tied them to the fence, grabbed their dry bags, waited for a gap in the traffic, sprinted across the road, climbed the fence and squelched across the paddock.

One end of the barn was stacked high with hay bales. The other end was taken up with an aluminium dinghy on a trailer, neatly stacked timber and fencing wire. They climbed up onto the bales and spread out their sleeping bags on the dry hay.

'Perhaps we should ask the farmer,' suggested Eddie.

Jack looked out at the grey sheets of rain sweeping across the paddock. 'Probably should.' The rain clattered on the tin roof above them. From the dry bag he pulled out the thermos and the sandwiches his dad had made for them that morning. 'As soon as it stops raining.'

'It always rains on our trips,' said Eddie.

'We had good weather on the Waikato trip,' said Jack.

'And it rained every day on the Whanganui trip,' said Eddie.

'Not all the time,' said Jack. 'There was a patch of blue sky at Pipiriki. The sun came out as were loading the kayaks back on dad's trailer.'

Eddie chomped through his second sandwich and looked at Jack.

'Engineering school is not a happening thing, is it?'

'It's okay for you; you know what you want.'

'Yep,' said Eddie, 'dentistry at Otago — you earn heaps.'

'Just because my dad and my grandad were doesn't mean I have to.'

'But you went to the open day.'

'I did, and it was fun. There was this professor bloke in a brown corduroy jacket. He gave us all a reel of cotton and a tube of glue, some thin strips of balsa wood and a brick and asked us to build a bridge that would hold the brick above two desks one metre apart. The lightest one would win a chocolate fish.

'I could see straightaway that the brick needed to be part of the structure, so I glued together two supports and connected them at the bottom with the cotton, like this.' Jack waved his hands in the air.

'Right,' said Eddie.

'I knew it would work as long as the cotton didn't snap.'

'So did it win the chocolate fish?'

'The professor bloke weighed it and said, "That's the second lightest one we've ever had." He gave me the chocolate fish and an application form to the engineering school. I promised to post it in.'

'But you haven't?'

'No.'

Jack cut the last sandwich in half.

After the engineering school they had visited the art school. In the painting studio a young woman in a leather jacket walked in with a roll of newsprint. She put it on the floor and gave it a kick; it slowly unrolled across the room. She asked the group to hold up the sides of the paper and then poured red paint at one end. The paint cascaded the length of the room, sloshing from side to side on the paper, breaking into separate streams, joining up again. Then she tipped some purple paint on and let it run down and mix with the red.

'Now pick your favourite bit of paint,' said the woman in the leather jacket. Jack pointed to where the paint had separated out like a river delta and spread across the paper.

'Why?' she asked.

Jack couldn't explain why; he just knew it was exciting. He liked the way she didn't care if paint splattered on the studio floor. He liked the vinegar smell of the chemicals in the photographic darkroom and the students' big charcoal drawings pinned on the white studio walls.

'Your portfolio is good enough. You'd get in,' his art teacher had said back at school.

The rain drummed on the barn roof. Jack poured the last of the tea into their plastic mugs. He turned to hand one to Eddie. Eddie was fast asleep.

The sketchbook

Jack's grandfather Sandy, Greenock, Scotland, 1931

YOU'LL BE OFF TO THE GLASGOW SCHOOL OF ART THEN.

JOHN G KINKAID
MARINE ENGINEERS

WELL, MAYBE NOT.

YEAH, MAYBE NOT.

The camera

Jack's grandfather Sandy, Greenock, Scotland, 1935

Sandy Tait started his apprenticeship in Kincaid's wearing his father's old overcoat. He finished it in the drawing office in 1935, wearing a white shirt and a Fair Isle jersey his mother had knitted. He'd done time in the boiler shop, the machine shop, the copper shop, the white-metal shop, the pattern shop and the finishing shop.

At lunchtime on his last day, he went to see Fiona Brodie in Kincaid's front office. Sandy's family sat in the pew behind the Brodie family in the Greenbank Church in Kelly Street. Sandy had spent every Sunday of his childhood listening to the Reverend McCrorie instructing the congregation that to work was to pray and sparing the rod would spoil the child and how the song would come tomorrow not today.

One Sunday when he was ten years old, as the Reverend explained that you should finish every meal feeling just a little hungry, he had untied the bow at the end of Fiona's long plait that fell over the back of the pew. 'Have we trials and temptations? Is there trouble anywhere?' He had gently looped the bow around the wooden bar that held up the hymn books. 'We should never be discouraged, take it to the Lord in prayer.' Then carefully knotted the bow again. 'Can we find a friend so faithful, who will all our sorrows share? ... We will now stand to sing "What a Friend We Have in Jesus".'

He could still remember Fiona's shriek.

Sandy's belief in the Reverend McCrorie disappeared the day that Billy's dad stepped back onto the second plank with his rivet gun. There was no second plank. There was no safety rail. Billy's dad had fallen 30 feet from the shipyard scaffolding onto the cobbles. The floral wreath from the company at his funeral was no compensation. The vague assurances from the Reverend McCrorie that Billy's dad had gone to a better place were no compensation. Sandy shifted his faith to Willie Gallacher and the shop stewards but kept going to church. He didn't want to argue with his parents.

Now he was free. The song would come today, not tomorrow.

'Are you away then?' asked Fiona.

'I hope so,' said Sandy. 'I was wanting to get a testimonial from the company.' Her hair was short these days and swung round her face.

'I'll type one up for you and get Mr Greer to sign it.' She rolled paper into her typewriter. 'And how's Billy doing?'

'Gone already,' said Sandy. 'He'll be in Halifax, Nova Scotia, by now, junior electrician on the *Trevanion*.'

Sandy's testimonial arrived in the mail two days later. There was a handwritten note tucked in with it: 'When you get a ship, you had better write to me, you great hair-pulling galoot! Fiona.'

A testimonial from the Reverend McCrorie arrived in the same post, saying that he knew Sandy Tait to be a young man of faith, integrity and reliability of character who would give more than reasonable satisfaction to anyone who employed him. Sandy raised an eyebrow at 'more than reasonable'.

Two weeks later he found he would be able to give more than reasonable satisfaction to the Elder Dempster shipping line when they offered him a position as a junior engineer on the *Accra*. He was to report to the ship at Liverpool the following Friday.

'So, you're sailing under the Red Duster,' said his father.

'The Red Duster?' said Sandy's mum, looking up from her knitting.

'The flag of the merchant fleet,' said his father.

His parents walked with him down Ann Street to the station to say goodbye. He knew that at the last moment his mother would abandon her Presbyterian reserve and give him a hug, but he wasn't sure about his father. Would he remain stern-faced and just nod? Would he shake his hand?

As they stood on the platform waiting for the train to leave, his father took his camera out of the pocket of his overcoat, unfolded it, and took a snap of Sandy and his mother.

The engine tooted. His mother said, 'Did you pack the scarf I knitted?' and gave him a tight hug. His father opened the carriage door with one hand and held out his other hand. Sandy reached out to shake it and realised his father was handing him his camera.

'You take this now you're off to see the world. We'll want to see the pictures when you get back.'

The guard blew his whistle. The train started to move.

The first photograph Sandy took was of the *Accra* at the Brunswick Dock in Liverpool. The second was from the top of the funnel as the ship pitched and tossed its way south. He liked the pattern the ventilator shafts made, each one looking at a different part of the horizon.

The hold was full of machinery and the cabins were full of Colonial Service administrators who had packed their children off to boarding school. Sandy was surprised to discover that the passengers all dressed for dinner. Nobody dressed for dinner in Greenock. As the *Accra* made its way down the coast of Africa and the weather got warmer, the passengers still put on their ties and dinner jackets. How did these people know the rules? he wondered, as he wiped his oily hands on his overalls.

At Port Harcourt in Nigeria, he took snaps of the wharf and of the Hausa men who came on board to trade carved wooden masks and brightly coloured cloth.

'When you come back, stick together,' said the chief engineer to Sandy and his mates as they headed down the gangway. 'The guards on the wharf gates will relieve you of your watch and wallet if you're on your own.'

Sandy left the others in a bar. I can see the inside of a bar in Greenock, he thought. He wandered around the market looking through the prism of the camera's viewfinder at women in turbans selling tomatoes, bananas and pineapples, and laughing children who tried to persuade him to take their photo. It seems safe enough, he thought.

When he arrived back at the wharf gates, it was dusk. The guard with the rifle that had smiled at them when they left had been joined by three others. He remembered the chief engineer's warning and stuffed the camera in his trouser pocket. He stopped in the middle of the road well back from the gate. The guards folded their arms and waited. He could see the stern of the *Accra* behind the wharf sheds. He was wondering what to do when a horn sounded. He turned and saw an ancient Morris truck approaching, and as the truck passed he leapt over the tailboard and lay flat. The truck stank of fish and cabbages. He'd jumped into the port rubbish truck.

He heard the guard shout. The truck stopped. He lifted his head and peered over the tailboard. They were through the gate, but the guard was running after the truck waving his rifle. Sandy leapt out and legged it around the corner of the wharf shed and up the *Accra*'s gangway.

'Phew!' said the second mate, holding his nose. 'Where have you been?'

Sandy felt in his pocket for the camera.

It was still there.

Lying on his bunk later that night, he wrote three letters home. The first was to his parents describing the storms in the Bay of Biscay, the

seasick passengers and the heat. He left out his ride in the rubbish truck.

The second letter was to Fiona. He described the surf boats rowing out to the ship and the traders climbing on board. He described the jungle at Sapele Creek as the *Accra* loaded logs. He left out what he really wanted to say.

The third was to Billy where he left nothing out at all.

The *Accra* returned to Liverpool loaded with tin and timber and district officers on leave. It sailed back up the Mersey on a still, wet morning to the Brunswick Dock. The journey had taken five weeks.

Back in Ann Street, he covered the kitchen window with a blanket to block out light from the street. He made sure no light was sneaking under the door from the hall and carefully mixed the photographic developer and the fixer. He loved the vinegar smell of the chemicals. He counted out the seconds as he exposed the photographic paper, then put the paper in the developer in one of his mother's baking dishes and watched the wharf at Port Harcourt and the Hausa traders slowly appear in the dim red glow of the safety light.

After he had been at home for two days, he called at Kincaid's office. It was an icy morning, but he was feeling hot and flustered as he walked up the steps. He was relieved to see Fiona was on her own behind the counter.

'I heard you were back.'

'Did you get my letter?'

'I did — the heat, the jungle, the traders, very good.'

Sandy suddenly couldn't remember all the nonchalant, witty conversation he had planned so he handed her the parcel without saying anything. She unfolded the paper and held up a square of bright red and orange material.

'I, um, I'm not sure if it's a scarf or a shawl or a turban,' he said, 'but I thought you might, well, you like bright colours and . . .'

Fiona wrapped the material around her shoulders. 'How does it look?'

'It looks grand,' said Sandy. 'It goes with your hair.'

She twirled around and laughed. 'And yes,' she said, 'this evening I would like to go and see *It Happened One Night* with Clark Gable and Claudette Colbert at the Regal. I'll meet you there at ten to eight. You will recognise me, I'll be wearing a red and orange shawl of African design.' She glanced at the open door behind her, 'And now you have to go. I have to get back to work before Mr Greer comes in to grumble that he is not paying me to gossip with corner boys.'

'Ten to eight,' she repeated as Sandy went back through the door.

Well, that was more than reasonable, thought Sandy as he walked back up Ann Street.

The following week Fiona invited him home for tea. Sandy gave her a box of chocolates as they walked towards her house.

'No, not me,' she whispered. 'Give them to my mum.'

Her mother was in the kitchen. Sandy nervously thrust the box of chocolates at her.

'Och, you shouldn't have,' she smiled. 'All the way from Africa?'

'All the way from the co-op in Cathcart Street,' said Sandy.

Her father was standing with his arms folded in front of the fireplace. Fiona's three younger sisters were sitting on the sofa. 'So you're stepping out with our Fiona then,' said her father.

'We're friends,' said Fiona.

'Well, you should make yourself at home then,' he said, offering Sandy his hand.

'That was a smart idea of yours to get me mum the chocolates,' whispered Fiona as he left.

Sandy had liked the way conversation in the Brodie household wasn't something you used only when you needed someone to pass the butter. He liked the way Mr Brodie would ask each of his daughters to describe the best thing that happened that day and then listen to what they said, and he liked the way they tried to outdo each other with their stories.

On Sunday after church, Sandy and Fiona walked up Ann Street. They didn't stop at Sandy's place. They kept on walking up to the moorland high above the town. They looked across The Tail of the Bank at the hills

on the far side of the river. They looked down at the shipyards with their tall cranes crowding the river's edge. A train tooted. There was a plume of smoke as it began its journey up the line to Glasgow. A new grey destroyer made its way down the river.

'Will you stay here?' asked Sandy.

'I'd like to get a job in Glasgow,' said Fiona. 'And you?'

'I'll work my way up,' said Sandy, 'to chief engineer.'

'And how long will that take?'

'Five years, maybe.'

'That's quite some time. Where is it you're away to next?

'I'm off on the *Taranaki*.'

'The what?'

'The *Taranaki*. My next ship, to Australia.'

'And how long will that take?'

'Five months.'

'Perhaps we should be heading back,' said Fiona. 'It's getting chilly.'

Sandy pushed his hands into his coat pockets and followed Fiona back down the path.

Two days out from the Panama Canal the number-six cylinder head valve exploded. The *Taranaki* came to a stop.

'How long?' asked the first officer.

'It'll take most of a day,' said the chief engineer.

All morning the ship sat still on a calm sea. In the middle of the afternoon the engine-room telegraph moved from stop to slow ahead. Sandy watched the main shaft slowly revolve. He listened to the regular chatter of the new valve like the tick of the grandfather clock in the hall back in Ann Street.

The broken valve was winched up onto the deck where Sandy carefully arranged the bent bolts and broken metal and took a photograph.

At the end of the watch, he lay on his bunk listening to the pleasing thrum of the ship's engine as it made its way on across the Pacific and tried to write to Fiona. He wanted to tell her about the explosion and how they got the ship going again, but his words got tangled up and banged into one another. If he'd grown up around a dining room table like the Brodies, where words were flung back and forth and poetry was read aloud, he might have learnt to put words down in a way that said what he wanted.

He tried the letter out on the third electrician. The third electrician looked doubtful.

'You and I, we think cylinder head valves are beautiful, and when they're all chattering away together it means we are a happy ship making our way across the ocean, but your Fiona — not so much. She won't know what a cylinder head valve looks like. Make it interesting lad, tell a story, "There we were stuck in the middle of the ocean not going anywhere", that sort of thing.'

He still hadn't got his letter written as the *Taranaki* sailed under the new Sydney Harbour Bridge. So much steel, marvelled Sandy, looking up. A train clattered over the bridge above the ship.

After the *Taranaki* had berthed in Darling Harbour, he had time to look around. He walked down George Street and around Circular Quay. I can't buy another shawl, he thought. He remembered how pleased Fiona's mother had been with the chocolates so he bought three small toy koala bears. One for each of Fiona's sisters: Florrie, Freya and Flora.

'I don't know,' Fiona had said. 'They liked Fs.'

The next stop was Port Melbourne. Over the railway tracks and the wharf sheds, past the stern of the *Melbourne Star* he saw the three elegant funnels of the *Empress of Britain*. It was the liner that Billy had drawn in his sketchbook as they made their way to work back in Greenock. He remembered Billy joking about going to art school.

Mail was waiting: two letters from his parents, one from Billy and one from Fiona. He opened Fiona's first. She told him about her new job in Glasgow. She told him how the yards were busy building ships for the navy. She told him about the sunny weather and then she said, 'Sandy, you are there and I am here, and I must be honest . . .'

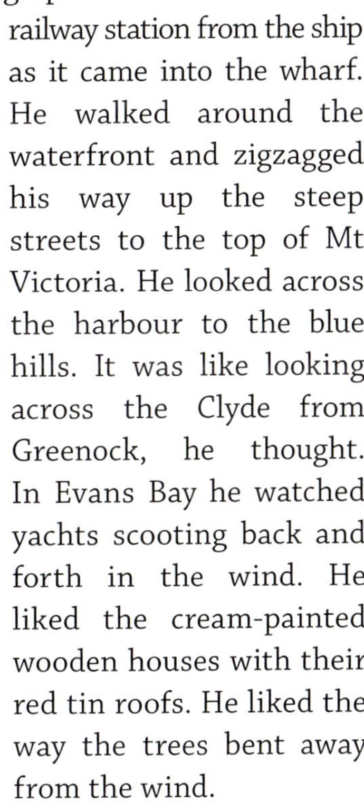

As the *Taranaki* steamed around the bottom of Australia to Fremantle, he spent hours on his own staring out at the grey Southern Ocean. One by one he hurled the stuffed koalas out into the greyness towards Antarctica.

His next ship was the *Karamea*, sailing out of London's Victoria Docks for New Zealand. Immigrants and machinery on the way out, mutton and wool on the way back. Sandy took photographs of his shipmates. Mr O'Malley and Mr Cooper put on their jackets. Kofi grinned directly at the camera. The plumber snoozed in the sun, oblivious to the click of the shutter. Sandy wrote their addresses in his notebook and promised to send prints.

On his first visit to Wellington, he photographed the new red-brick railway station from the ship as it came into the wharf. He walked around the waterfront and zigzagged his way up the steep streets to the top of Mt Victoria. He looked across the harbour to the blue hills. It was like looking across the Clyde from Greenock, he thought. In Evans Bay he watched yachts scooting back and forth in the wind. He liked the cream-painted wooden houses with their red tin roofs. He liked the way the trees bent away from the wind.

The wrong tram

Jack's grandmother Mary, Berlin, 1935

Mary Penwarden pushed open the glass doors of Wertheim's department store and stepped onto the pavement. Boys in uniform were standing in front of the store windows holding signs.

'Look, Auntie, a parade.'

Aunt Adina grabbed Mary's hand, bundled her down Leipziger Platz onto the first tram that came by.

'It's the wrong tram,' said Mary. 'It's going the wrong way.'

'Nothing's going the right way,' muttered Aunt Adina.

WERTHEIM
WERTHEIM
WERTHEIM
WERTHEIM
JUDEN

‘What did the signs say?’ asked Mary, looking back out of the tram window. She thought the boys looked smart in their ironed shirts.

She decided not to show Aunt Adina the poster she had folded up in the bottom of her suitcase.

A week later when she arrived back home in London, she unfolded the poster and pinned it up on her bedroom wall. It had been there for three days when her mother came into her room and said, ‘There won’t be any more holidays with Aunt Adina.’

Mary put down her book. 'Why?'

'We are trying to get her to come and live here.'

'Why does she need to come here?'

Her mother pointed at the poster. 'It's your folk in their brown uniforms. They don't like people like Auntie Adina,' she paused and added, 'people like us. They're building a navy again and conscripting an army.'

'Will Auntie be alright?'

'If we can get a passport and a visa,' said her mother. 'We want her here.'

When her mother had gone, Mary Penwarden took the poster down, folded it up and put it in the drawer of her bedside table.

The kangaroo in the kitbag

Jack's grandfather Sandy, Townsville, Australia, 1939

The cook untied the top of his kitbag. A kangaroo stuck its head out.

'Is that for breakfast?' asked Sandy.

'I'm not eating no kangaroo,' said Freddy Revel.

The cook couldn't remember how he acquired the kangaroo. He couldn't remember much of his shore leave or how he got back to the *Mahia* from Buchanan's Hotel.

'It's not a kangaroo,' said the third electrician. 'It's a wallaby, a baby wallaby.'

The *Mahia* sailed from Townsville that evening with the wallaby still aboard. By the time the ship was halfway across the Pacific, Joey had been promoted to Catering Storekeeper 1st Class.

'That kangaroo is getting fat,' said Sandy to the cook one evening, as they watched Joey hopping around the deck.

'He's only on light duties,' replied the cook, feeding him another carrot from a tin. 'Got to fatten him up. He'll have a ration book when he gets home. We'll all have ration books.'

'Could he handle a paintbrush?' asked Freddy Revel.

'Not Catering Department duties,' said the cook.

'We've got to finish painting this ship grey before we reach Panama.'

'Even the brass work?' asked Sandy.

'Even the brass,' said Freddy. 'We don't want nothing shiny, no more polishing for the duration of the war.'

The last to go were the cream and black Shaw Savill and Albion Line colours on the funnel.

When they were through the Panama Canal, they joined thirty-three other merchant ships all painted the same dull grey.

'We're like one of the Reverend McCrorie's sermons,' thought Sandy, as they zigzagged their way up the Atlantic escorted by six old destroyers.

'Why so many altogether?' asked the third electrician.

'It gives the other team a sporting chance to hit something when they find us,' said the cook. 'Joey and I should have stayed at Buchanan's Hotel.'

The weather was dull and grey and wet, and the U-boats didn't find them in the Atlantic storms. The sun came out as they sailed around the north of Ireland.

In two days' time, I'll be back in the kitchen at Ann Street printing my photographs, thought Sandy.

On the last night at sea, a submarine slipped unseen into the centre of the convoy and raised its periscope. It was a fine night with a full moon. There were four bright orange flashes. Four explosions. Four merchant ships sank. Some of the sailors made it to the lifeboats. Many did not. The other ships did not stop to pick up survivors. Any ship that stopped would become a target.

'How was it?' asked Sandy's mother, as they walked up Ann Street from the station.

'Townsville was sunny,' he said.

Once around the rose garden

Jack's grandmother Mary, London, 1939

A letter came through the front door. Mary picked it up off the tiles. She recognised the handwriting — it was hers. She had to get her German dictionary to check the translation of the red stamp across the envelope. Aunt Adina was 'No longer at this address'.

She showed the letter to her mother, who stopped peeling the potatoes and put her head in her hands.

A week later as she was drying the dishes, she said to her parents, 'I'm not returning for my second year at secretarial college.' Her father put down the dish-mop and looked at her.

'I've joined the navy.'

'The Wrens,' said her mother.

'Yes, the Wrens.'

'Why?'

Mary looked at the letter to Aunt Adina sitting on the mantelpiece. 'I liked the hat.'

Mary spent her first two weeks in the navy in a cold house in Wimbledon practising Morse code. A young man with a blue polo-neck jersey and a walking stick sent the Morse code from one end of the dining room table. Mary sat with six other women around the huge table and listened to it on headphones. She wrote down the dots and dashes on a pad. The man with the walking stick would limp around the table and look at their notepads, sit back down, turn up the static to make the Morse harder to hear, and increase the speed. At the end of the fortnight Mary sat an exam.

'We're sending you to a golf club in Cornwall,' said the man who sent the Morse.

'I don't play golf,' said Mary.

'We've taken it over. It's now a Y station.'

'What's a Y station?'

'You listen to enemy radio messages.'

'Like spying?'

'Sort of.'

Mary had a weekend's leave before taking the train to Cornwall. On Saturday morning her mother brought her a cup of tea and sat on the end of the bed.

'A good thing you did the Morse code with the Guides.'

'Yes, we listen in to messages from —' Mary slapped her hand over her mouth. 'I can't tell you. I had to sign the Official Secrets Act.'

Her mother smiled. 'Can you tell me if you still take sugar?'

The train to Cornwall was crowded with sailors, soldiers and bewildered children carrying cardboard boxes tied with string. Mary had to sit on her suitcase in the corridor. No one met her when she got off. She sat in the waiting room. After ten minutes a lorry pulled up. A voice called out, 'Come for the golf?' Mary grabbed her bag and went to climb in the back of the lorry. 'Not in there, here in the front. My name's Sheila,' said the driver. 'We don't go much on that saluting business. There are all sorts — scientists in cardigans, professors from the university. You'll like it.'

The Y station had four new radio towers, one at each corner of the clubhouse. In the long grass by the ninth tee was a wooden tower that looked like a windmill without sails. 'That's the direction finder,' said Sheila.

Mary spent her shifts searching the airwaves on her high-frequency radio. Occasionally in the clutter of sounds she would hear cab drivers in New York, but what she really wanted were Morse-code messages

from U-boats. There would be long hours of nothing and then brief transmissions. Some operators would bang out messages on the Morse key in staccato bursts and others would caress the key gently. Mary came to recognise the stroke of one operator in particular who tapped lightly and always lingered on the last keystroke. Her shifts were changed to coincide with his. Did he look like the boys she had seen outside Wertheim's department store? she wondered.

After a long period when she hadn't been able to find him, she picked up a quick, clear transmission late one evening. She jotted down the message and pressed the button on her desk. The duty sergeant hurried over and collected the list of dots and dashes scribbled on her pad.

In a wooden hut surrounded by four tall radio masts in Thurso in the north of Scotland, another listener picked up the same message. The direction it came from was plotted. The two lines crossed in the middle of the Atlantic, showing it was sent from a U-boat shadowing a convoy sailing into The Gap, the area where the convoys of merchant ships were outside the range of protecting aircraft.

'What happens to these people I listen to?' asked Mary.

'We assist them to change their line of work,' said the duty sergeant.

When they weren't working, Sheila and Mary would walk around the overgrown golf course. One evening they took a rusty spade leaning against the greenkeeper's shed and levered open the door. Inside in the dim light they could see dust-covered hand mowers, hedge clippers, rakes and bags of golf clubs. There was a large mowing machine with an empty space in front of it.

'The tractor must have been requisitioned,' said Sheila, 'like us.' In a drawer of the greenkeeper's workbench Mary found a book — *The Rules of the Game of Golf*. She opened the book and read, 'The green should be closely mown to create a smooth surface suitable for putting.'

'It seems a pity to waste a perfectly good golf course,' she said, stuffing the book in her pocket. They trundled a push mower down the overgrown fairway to the first green and started mowing.

'Rhythm and balance are essential for a good swing. If done correctly, you should begin to add distance to your drive,' advised *The Rules of the Game of Golf*. By the end of summer Mary's swing had rhythm, balance and drive.

In between games of golf, they sat in the clubhouse for long hours listening for messages from U-boats in the Atlantic and Italian torpedo boats in the Mediterranean.

Dispatch riders on Triumph motorcycles raced away down the drive with the messages they recorded. Mary and Sheila were finishing their morning cup of tea in the sun on the front steps of the

clubhouse as one of the motorcyclists packed her pannier bags.

'How about a ride?' asked Sheila.

'Okay,' said the dispatch rider. 'Once round the rose garden.' Sheila squeezed onto the seat behind the driver. Laughing, they circled the overgrown rose garden. 'Where do you take our messages?' she asked.

'A country house called —'

'Stop!' shouted Mary. 'Remember Brenda, who had too much to drink at a party and talked about what she did at Bletchley Park? The military police took her away — she's never been seen again.' The dispatch rider laughed, pulled down her goggles, and roared away down the driveway.

Casting off

Sandy and Billy, Greenock, July 1941

Sandy leant over his mother's shoulder and read her knitting pattern: 'If you can knit you can do your bit, keep the men in the services smiling, knit them woollies. This pullover can be worn under almost any uniform and should be found in all kitbags.'

His mother had a wooden ruler marking the line she was up to: 'Commence at the lower edge with number nine needles casting on one hundred and eight stitches. Knit one, purl one, for twenty-two rows.'

'Where is it this time?' asked his mother.

'They don't tell us.'

'There's one pullover for you and one for Billy. I'll have them sewn up by the morning.'

'What does "pass the slipped stitch over" mean?' Sandy asked.

'It means you'll be warm,' said his mother.

'I'll be warm as toast down in the engine room.'

'What if you're on one of those convoys that go around the top of Norway to Russia?' said his mother.

'You're not supposed to know about them.'

His mother's knitting needles clattered on.

'All we know is that we report to a ship called the *Sydney Star* in Liverpool. We catch the train down tomorrow morning.'

'You and Billy.'

'Me and Billy.'

'You bring Billy back.'

'I'll bring Billy back,' said Sandy. 'Promise.'

Moira Tait and Billy's mum walked back up Ann Street from the station.

'You'll be coming in for a cup of tea then.'

'I will.'

'We've got a banana.'

'It's a long time since I've seen a banana,' said Moira.

'It's from one of those American Liberty ships.'

The banana was sitting in the middle of the mantelpiece.

'Billy said it's getting ripe.'

Moira poured the milk into the teacups.

'Do you think we should?'

'It is getting ripe.'

Billy's mum carefully cut the banana in two and put each half on a plate. 'I do hope it's not one of those convoys to Russia,' she said. 'It would be so cold. If something happened to Billy, there would only be me left.'

When she arrived back home Moira started knitting: 'With number ten needles commence at the cuff casting on forty-four stitches. Knit in a rib of knit two, purl two for three inches.'

She moved her wooden ruler down to the next row on the knitting pattern. When the mittens were finished, she would put them in the post.

'Half the frigging roof is missing!' said Billy as they stepped onto the Liverpool Station platform. Sandy looked up — where there had been a beautiful arch of steel and glass, there was now sky through twisted blackened beams. They grabbed their bags from the luggage rack and hurried out to the tram stop.

'Half the frigging city is missing,' said Sandy as their tram made its way past a burnt-out department store. Rubble from collapsed buildings had been pushed to the side of the road to clear tramlines. Office workers hurrying home picked their way over piles of bricks. A double-decker bus

lay on its side in a park. An undamaged piano stood in the middle of the pavement. They found their way to Mrs Flowerday's lodging house in Errol Street and knocked on the front door.

There were three places set at one table next morning.

'Mr Crosby will be joining you,' said Mrs Flowerday. 'You'll like him.' Sandy didn't see why he had to like Mr Crosby or why Mr Crosby couldn't have breakfast at his own table and leave him and Billy to read the paper.

'There's porridge, but no eggs. Eggs are hard to get.' Mrs Flowerday poured Billy and Sandy cups of tea.

'I'll bring you some eggs next time,' said a naval officer, hanging his coat on the back of the chair.

'That would be very nice, Mr Crosby.'

'We like to keep you happy, Mrs Flowerday.'

Sandy looked over the top of his newspaper.

'Crosby, Ben Crosby,' said the naval officer, thrusting his hand across the table.

'Sandy Tait and that's Billy Preston.'

'And what did you do before Mr Hitler began the current unpleasantness?' Billy asked.

'Greek,' said Ben Crosby.

Here we go, a senior service smart aleck, thought Sandy and went back to his newspaper.

'It was a toss-up between that or Icelandic,' said Ben Crosby, then he added, 'at university.' Sandy recognised Ben Crosby's accent. 'Do they speak Greek in New Zealand?'

Ben Crosby laughed. 'I arrived in 1938 on a scholarship. When Mr Hitler invaded Poland, the navy mistook my ability to sail a dinghy as a qualification so here I am, Sub-Lieutenant Crosby of the destroyer *Fearless*, which is not quite as comfortable as Mrs Flowerday's.' Mrs Flowerday placed a tray with toast, marmalade and porridge on the table.

'Where did you learn to sail?' asked Sandy.

'In Wellington Harbour.'

'Evans Bay?'

'Yes. You've been there?'

Sandy nodded, 'It's a bit breezy.'

'Well, I tipped over a lot, ended up on the rocks sometimes. If you could stay upright, it was fun.'

'Will you go back?'

'I'd like to finish my studies and then go back. I'll miss the newspapers and the theatre and the galleries and all that, but, yes, it's home. Next time you're there, when all this is over, you should look me up. I'll take you out for a sail — just stick your head in the door of the Evans Bay Yacht Club.'

'Yacht clubs and universities aren't for the likes of us,' said Billy.

'It's not like that. You can knock up a dinghy in your garage.'

'You've got a garage?'

'It was my dad's — he had to leave the Morrie out on the street all winter.'

'So Jack's as good as his master,' said Sandy. 'I could give that a try.'

'When we get our lives back,' said Billy.

'When we get our lives back,' agreed Ben. 'In the meantime I have to report to the good ship *Fearless*.' He gulped the last of his tea and stood up. 'See you next time, Mrs F.'

'With some eggs, Mr C.'

'He was alright,' said Billy when they had finished their second cups of tea.

Sandy folded the newspaper.

On the bridge of the *Sydney Star* Captain Horn looked through his cargo manifest. If this lot is hit, he thought, it's going to be a very big bang. He also had to squeeze in 484 artillerymen. He hadn't been told where the convoy was going, but based on the list in front of him, he could make a reasonable guess.

The following day at noon he eased the *Sydney Star* out of the Birkenhead docks into the River Mersey. There he joined three other merchant ships: the *City of Pretoria*, the *Port Chalmers* and

OPERATION SUBSTANCE

Kerosene 2661 tons, MT spirit 708 tons,
coal 4791 tons, cement 2660 tons
Foodstuffs (tons): fodder 989, tinned fish 291,
tinned veg 755, flour 1600, wheat 5345,
maize 680, rice 240, margarine 212, butter 25,
edible oil 196, cheese 101, coffee 134
Colonial Office: stores 151 tons
Medical stores: 46 tons
Stationery: 12 tons
Mail: 197.5 tons
Ammunition 290000 rounds, bombs 61000,
grenades 45000, smoke bombs 12300,
signal flares 105000, explosive 72000 lbs,
detonators 25000, cord 90000 ft,
mine fuzes & detonators 16400.
Mobile guns 20, Bren guns 75,
rifles 3245, guns 7853
Vehicles:
anti-aircraft tractors 29, Bren carriers 30,
motor cycles 84, pedal cycles 70, lories 24,
trailers 20, winch 1, fire engine 1,
RAF tractors 12
Motor transport stores: 331 tons
Naval power boats 3, seaplane tender 1
NAAFI: stores 1376 tons
Naval Armament (tons): stores 1107,
victualling 740, general supplies 761
Ordnance: stores 2975 tons
Royal Air Force (tons):
stores 779, ammunition 397, oil 198,
aviation spirit 5187
Royal Army Ordnance Corps: stores 11 tons
Royal Engineers: stores 708 tons
Bomb Disposal: equipment 2 tons
General supplies 4704 tons

the *Deucalion*. They steamed down the river out into the Irish Sea.

He looked through his binoculars at the two navy destroyers that had joined them, the *Van Heemskerck* and the *Fearless*, and wondered who was in charge. He flashed a signal ordering the ships to form a port column at three cables from the *Sydney Star*. To his surprise they swung into line.

Later in the afternoon they were joined by more merchant ships, two cruisers, the battleship *Nelson*, and the battlecruiser *Renown*. Captain Horn was pleased to be relieved of his position as convoy commodore. They sailed out into the Atlantic for two days. When they were out of range of the Germans' Condor bombers, they turned south.

'Where do you think we're headed?' asked Sandy as he stirred two spoonfuls of sugar into his cup of tea.

'South Africa, I reckon,' said Frank Bones the carpenter. Mr Machie the chief officer and George Haig the chief engineer disagreed.

'Right around the Cape to India,' they insisted.

The Royal Navy will assist you

Sandy and Billy, the Sydney Star, July 1941

Five days later Sandy and Billy watched a destroyer they hadn't seen before dash from ship to ship firing a rocket line with a package onto each ship.

'Whatever that is, it's so important they don't want to say it over the radio,' said Billy, 'and that ship firing the rockets, she's from the Mediterranean.'

'How can you tell?' asked Sandy.

'The lighter grey paint,' said Billy. 'Gibraltar, probably.'

When he came up from the engine room at the end of his watch, Sandy was able to read the message. Captain Horn had it displayed throughout the ship.

'The trouble is,' said Mr Machie, 'the Italians will know about this great mission before it's started. There are French spies watching from the African coast and Italian spies watching from the Spanish coast. They'll be on the blower to Benito before we're through the Straits of Gibraltar.'

BLUE STAR LINE

For over twelve months Malta has resisted all attacks of the enemy. The gallantry displayed by the garrison and the people of Malta has aroused admiration throughout the world. To enable their defense to be continued, it is essential that your ships with their valuable cargoes should arrive safely in Grand Harbour.

The Royal Navy will assist you in this great mission; you in your turn can assist the Royal Navy by giving strict attention to the following points: Don't make smoke. Don't show any lights at night. Keep good station. Don't straggle. If your ship is damaged keep her going by the best possible speed.

At midnight on 21 July the convoy sailed through the straits in thick fog. They couldn't be seen by anyone. Captain Horn's only difficulty was seeing the ship in front. When the fog lifted the next morning, he found the aircraft carrier *Ark Royal* and more warships from the British naval base at Gibraltar had joined them.

'Another sunny Mediterranean holiday,' sighed Frank Bones, looking out at the flat sea and the cloudless sky, as they raced east along the African coast, the big warships to the north to fight off bombers flying from Sardinia.

The cruiser *Manchester*, concerned that the *Port Chalmers* was lagging behind, flashed her a signal: 'S stands for straggler and for sunk.'

'Perhaps they're on holiday too,' said Mr Machie, as the sun set behind them. 'Maybe our Mediterranean cruise will make it.'

Next morning an Italian spotter plane circled the navy ships to the north, taking care to stay out of range.

'Holiday over,' said Frank Bones.

All day they scanned the sky waiting for the bombers. None came, and for a second night they were wrapped in a protective cloak of darkness.

As Sandy was coming on watch on the third morning, he saw the big guns on the warships swivel around to the north. He watched a Fulmar fighter lumber along the deck of the aircraft carrier *Ark Royal*. He couldn't believe it had enough speed to lift off, but it did, and others followed. He watched the Fulmars disappear in the direction the guns were pointing.

Then, without warning, a group of torpedo bombers came racing out of the east with the morning sun behind them.

Sandy watched a torpedo slam into the *Manchester*. Seconds later another hit the *Fearless*. A huge column of black smoke billowed up. Sandy ran for the engine room.

Don't think about what's happening up there, he told himself, keep the engines running. He remembered the *Taranaki* sitting still for a whole day in the middle of the Pacific as they repaired the cylinder head valve. If the *Sydney Star*'s engines stopped now they would

be sunk. There would be little chance of making it up the engine room ladder. As the morning went on, the guns above thumped into action twice more. There were no violent, evasive swerves. The attacks must have been driven off.

'We've still got to get through Bomb Alley,' said Frank Haigh.

'What's Bomb Alley?' asked Sandy.

'The Skerki Channel, the shallows between Sicily and Tunisia. The big warships turn back. It's too dangerous for them to run Bomb Alley; it's like lining up in a shooting gallery. We'll be on our own.'

They weren't totally on their own. They had an escort of destroyers and the Fulmars from the *Ark Royal* overhead as they raced through the channel into the safety of the oncoming night.

On the bridge of the *Sydney Star*, Captain Horn and the first mate could hear bombers flying south. They could see flares lighting up the African coast.

Captain Horn turned the *Sydney Star* north.

WE'RE STEAMING INTO THE PANTELLERIA MINEFIELD.

ALWAYS GO WHERE THE ENEMY LEAST SUSPECTS, MR MACHIE.

BY TWO IN THE MORNING THE ISLAND OF PANTELLERIA WAS BEHIND THEM.

ONLY 150 MILES TO MALTA.

SUDDENLY OUT IN THE DARKNESS POWERFUL MOTORS ROARED INTO LIFE.

TORPEDO BOATS!

A torpedo slammed into the *Sydney Star*. The ship lurched sideways. Sandy was thrown to the floor. The engines juddered to a halt. The lights went out. She'll break in half, he thought, as he fumbled around on the floor for his torch.

The lights flickered back on.

'Good work, Billy.'

'It hit number three,' yelled Frank Bones. They clambered into number three hold. Looking down, they saw a forty-foot hole in the side of the ship. Water poured in.

'There's at least thirty feet of it,' said Sandy.

'We can shore up those buckled plates. You get the pumps started.'

Up on the bridge Captain Horn ordered the artillerymen to prepare to abandon ship. They lined up beside the lifeboats, even though those on the starboard side were smashed by gunfire.

The Italian boats, out of ammunition and torpedoes, had disappeared into the darkness.

The ship had drifted close to Pantelleria when the Australian Navy destroyer *Nestor* found it. Captain Rosenthal eased the *Nestor* alongside. Planks were laid. It took half an hour for all the troops and most of the crew from the *Sydney Star* to cross to the *Nestor.*

Out in the darkness they heard torpedo boats return to search for them.

'We're not finished yet,' Captain Horn told Captain Rosenthal on the *Nestor.* 'We're only a hundred and twenty miles from Malta.' George Haig and Sandy fired up the engines. An hour before daylight both ships were under way at a speed of ten knots. When the sun rose, they were over the horizon out of sight.

Captain Horn knew it was only a temporary escape. Searching planes would soon find them and now he had no gunners to protect his ship. During the night when it was thought the ship was sinking, they had all crossed to the *Nestor.* Over the ship's intercom he called for volunteers. Billy stuck his head out from behind a tangle of electrical cables and looked at Mr Machie.

Mr Machie pointed to a machine gun out on the wing of the bridge. He was joined by Joe who came running up from the stokehold.

'What do you know about machine guns?' asked Mr Machie.

Billy looked at Joe. Joe looked at the gun and scratched his head.

'The general idea is one of you points the gun at the approaching planes and presses this firing button here and the other one feeds in the ammunition,' said Mr Machie. 'End of lesson. Best of luck.' He hurried off to the two greasers looking doubtfully at their gun on the opposite wing of the bridge.

'I'm a stoker — I'll shovel in the ammunition,' said Joe.

Billy swung the gun around and pointed it at the horizon and there, coming towards them out of the rising sun, were two tiny black dots. The *Nestor* lowered its big guns and pointed them at the approaching planes. They banged into action. Explosions filled the sky around the bombers. On they came, weaving slowly left and right, trying to avoid the exploding shells.

'What's the range of this thing?' Billy shouted.

'Let's find out!' yelled Joe. Billy pressed the firing button. The gun thundered into life, bucking and juddering. The noise was deafening. The bombers came steadily on. Billy could now see their propellers whirling. A torpedo dropped with a splash and came scything through the water.

'That kipper is coming straight for us,' yelled Joe. The ship swerved violently and heeled over. The torpedo slipped past the *Sydney Star*'s stern.

At seven o'clock, a lone bomber dropped another torpedo that exploded in the *Sydney Star*'s wake.

At seven-thirty, two more bombers approached. The *Nestor*'s guns kept them at a safe distance.

At eight o'clock, Captain Horn was relieved to see the anti-aircraft cruiser *Hermione* come racing back from the convoy to join them.

Frank Bones measured the water flooding in. There was now sixteen feet of water in hold number one, seven feet in hold number two and forty-six feet of water in hold number three. Water was pouring in faster than it could be pumped out. The ship was listing to starboard and becoming hard to steer.

At half past ten a new group of low-level torpedo bombers came skimming over the waves. At the same time, 13,000 feet above the three ships, a group of high-level bombers opened their bomb doors and let loose their deadly cargo.

Billy and Joe aimed their machine gun at the approaching torpedo bombers. Again, the bombers came doggedly on and again they watched a torpedo splash into the water and slice towards them. Too full of water to make sudden turns, the *Sydney Star* just kept its course, and the torpedo snaked past the bow. The bomber flashed over the ship. Billy swung the gun around after it and stitched a neat row of bullet holes through the *Sydney Star*'s funnel.

A group of dive-bombers came screaming down out of the sun. Three bombs exploded beside the ship. A vast column of water shot skyward

and then came cascading down, drenching them. The ship heeled over and wallowed in the turmoil. The engines stopped.

The empty bombers turned and headed back to Sicily, followed by wild, erratic gunfire from the *Sydney Star*'s enthusiastic new gunners that went on long after the planes were out of range. Joe grabbed Billy's arm and pulled it off the firing button. He shook Billy by the hand. Billy could see Joe was saying something, but he couldn't hear what it was. He had been deafened by the noise of the gun.

Back in the engine room Frank Bones and Sandy propped and wedged every bit of timber they could find against the bulkhead. They knew that if it collapsed there would be no escape from the wall of water that would come crashing in. They restarted the engines.

It was eighteen miles to Malta. Captain Horn checked his charts to see if there were any sites where he could beach the ship. He could take it slowly and give the bulkheads time to collapse or he could go full steam ahead and risk the vibration and the water sloshing back and forth collapsing them. He had not slept for three days. Was he thinking clearly?

He put his hand on the engine-room telegraph and looked at Mr Machie. Mr Machie nodded. He moved the handle from slow to full ahead.

At ten past two in the afternoon the *Sydney Star* entered Malta's Grand Harbour.

BLIMEY, IT'S LIKE BLACKPOOL ON BANK HOLIDAY WEEKEND.
ALL THE CARGO SHIPS GOT THROUGH.

WE MADE IT.
HOME SAFE.

The lady with the alligator purse

Jack's grandmother Mary, London, 1941

Mary Penwarden stood on the street in front of her house. The street she had played in as a girl. She remembered her friends and their skipping rhymes.

I am a Girl Guide dressed in blue
These are the actions I must do
Salute to the Captain, bow to the Queen
Turn my back on the boys in green.

She would sing with the other girls as they swung the rope in the middle of the road. She remembered her mother opening their blue front door and calling her in for dinner.

'But I'm not out yet,' she would call back, and the girls would swing the rope faster.

Salt
mustard
vinegar
pepper . . .

As the girls grew older the rhymes changed.

Cinderella dressed in yella
Went upstairs to kiss a fella
Made a mistake and kissed a snake
How many doctors did it take
1, 2, 3, 4 . . .

Then the rhymes were forgotten, and Mary and her friends walked over the railway bridge to the Methodist Church Hall and became real Girl Guides. She liked the big blue hat and the white lanyard and the leather belt and badges: First Aid, Pathfinder, Morse Code, Lifesaver.

Later still she began to spend her summer holidays with Aunt Adina in Berlin. She

remembered the returned letter and wondered where her aunt was now.

At her feet was a broken milk bottle, and the milk had left a white stain on the road. Her blue front door was lying in the middle of the road. There were bricks and roof tiles and splintered window frames and smashed furniture on the footpath. Mary recognised a burnt corner of her bedspread.

She wondered what had happened to the poster of the girl with the golden plaits and the brown uniform that she had brought back from Berlin and left folded up in the drawer of her bedside table. She wondered what had happened to the bedside table.

'You can't go in, love,' said the constable standing at the front gate.

'I grew up there,' said Mary.

'There's nothing — it all went up in smoke and anything left was nicked by the looters.' The constable pushed back his helmet and looked at her.

'Oh heck,' he said, 'so you . . .'

'Buried them yesterday,' said Mary. She turned and walked back over the railway bridge, past the Methodist Church Hall to the station.

Mother, mother, I am ill
Call for the doctor over the hill
In came the doctor
In came the nurse
In came the lady with the alligator purse
'Measles,' said the doctor
'Mumps,' said the nurse
'Dead,' said the lady with the alligator purse.

Is my English listener listening?

Jack's grandmother Mary, Cornwall, 1945

When Mary was listening for submarines, she heard scrambled Morse code. When she was listening to aircraft, she heard the language she had learnt with Aunt Adina.

One morning a pilot reporting his position added, 'And is my English listener listening?' Minutes later she heard his plane accelerate, the sound of gunfire, then the plane diving.

'Bail out!' Mary yelled at her radio.

The pilot screamed all the way down.

There was a crash.

An explosion.

Silence.

Mary was tired. She was tired of death. She was tired of being cold and eating rhubarb. She was tired of wearing the cardigan she had been wearing since 1940. She had no home to go back to. She looked at the world map pinned to the wall. Little paper flags had been stuck in to mark the front line moving across Europe: June 1944, the D-Day landings; August 1944, Paris liberated; Christmas 1944, the failed counter-attack in the Ardennes; January 1945, Soviet troops enter Auschwitz. Mary knew now that boys in brown shirts would have rounded up Aunt Adina and crammed her into a cattle wagon and taken her to a camp like Auschwitz.

Soon the war would end. There would be nothing to listen for. Sheila was planning to go to Montreal with the captain of a corvette. Mary didn't like the sound of the freezing winters. What about those islands away down in the bottom right-hand corner of the map — perhaps it would be warm there?

From the rail of the steamship *Rangitikei*, Mary watched England disappear — the Cornwall coast a low grey smudge in the rain. She wondered if the radio towers at the golf club had been dismantled and the putting greens and the fairways were neatly mowed again.

'Goodbye to all that,' she said to the man at the rail next to her. She looked at his overcoat.

'The Grey Funnel line?' she asked.

'No, the Red Duster.'

‘Fun?’

‘Nothing exciting,’ said the man in the coat. ‘The only fun we had was our kangaroo. We kidnapped him in Australia — he sailed back to England with us, our mascot like, kept us safe.’

‘And what happened to your kangaroo? Was he discharged with a chest full of medals at the end of his war service?’

‘Found him on deck one morning behind a pile of timber. Must have died of fright during the night.’

‘Nothing exciting?’

The man in the coat didn’t answer. Land’s End disappeared into the greyness.

‘It’s getting chilly. Let’s go inside,’ she said.

Sandy pushed his hands into his coat pockets and followed. ‘What did you do?’ he asked.

‘Typist,’ said Mary.

Wait for me

Jack's dad Alec, Wellington, 1956

'Take Alec with you for once,' said Mary. She held up Alec's coat — he stuffed his arms in the sleeves then pulled on his mittens. Sandy put down the *Evening Post* and looked at their boy standing by the kitchen table. 'I'll go on my own,' he said. 'It's going to rain.'

'He wants to come with you.'

'Okay, we'll take the tram.'

Alec stood on the wooden seat and looked at the city. He liked the tram. He liked the way it swayed and clattered, he liked the swinging leather straps hanging from the roof, and he liked the way the wheels screeched when it went around the big corner on Pirie Street. His father gave him the pennies to give to the tram conductor.

They got off at the railway station. His father held his hand as they crossed the road to the wharf gates. They walked along the wharf past sheds full of wool bales and rail wagons full of frozen mutton carcasses in muslin bags. Men were loading the mutton carcasses into a rope sling on the wharf. When the sling was full a crane, which looked like the one in the book that came with his Meccano set, hoisted the mutton up over the side of a ship.

'Where's that ship from?' Alec asked.

'London. Liverpool maybe.'

'What's it called?'

'The *Sydney Star*,' said his father, without looking up at the name.

'Whose ship is it?'

SHIPS & SAILORS

By Wayfarer

The 11,219-ton Blue Star Line vessel Sydney Star, now berthed at Pipitea Wharf, was 15 years ago one of the central actors in a desperate real life drama.

In July, 1941, the Admiralty called for volunteer crews for her along with four vessels, on a mission which was described as "life and death." The Mediterranean was at its most dangerous for Allied shipping, and much of the course of this convoy lay within reach of the shore-based German and Italian bombers. U-boats were everywhere and E-boats a constant menace.

The Sydney Star had on board more than 600 troops and other important supplies. She was accompanied by the Melbourne Star, City of Pretoria, Turham and Teucallion and escorted by 10 cruisers, the battleships Nelson and Rodney and 32 destroyers.

After leaving Gibraltar on the last leg of the journey, the convoy was bombed continuously and the first casualty was one of the escorting destroyers which was so badly damaged it had to be sunk by gunfire. The next casualty was the cruiser Manchester, which with 200 troops on board was badly hit and had to return to Gibraltar,

At 3 a.m. on the fifth day, the convoy was attacked by enemy submarines and E-boats. With a shattering explosion, the Sydney Star was hit in the No. 3 hold by a torpedo which tore a hole 40 feet wide by 30 feet deep in the ship's side. A second torpedo skimmed underneath the hull, missing by only a few feet.

The ship's speed immediately dropped from 15 to 10 knots and as two of the destroyers raced to take some of the troops off, shore batteries began firing on the ship. About three boatloads of troops were sent across and then the Australian destroyer Nestor came alongside and the rest of the troops crossed over to her.

Escorted by one cruiser and seven destroyers the crippled Sydney Star made for the safety of Malta, reaching there after more dive-bomber attacks.

The convoy sailed on and eventually reached its destination without more losses in spite of repeated attacks. On the return journey, however, the Turham was sunk at Gibraltar by a limpet mine placed by the same Italian frogmen who damaged a British warship in the first frogman attack of the war

On entering Malta harbour the Sydney Star was beached, one, two and three holds being completely flooded. After a while she was pumped dry and put on the dock. During this time she was bombed on an average of eight times a day and during the six months that the Sydney Star was in Malta, the number of raids rose by 864.

After a period on the dock it was found that the Sydney Star could not have the insulation material in the damaged refrigerated holds replaced and she sailed through the Suez Canal for Durban and then to Buenos Aires, where she stayed for another six months before being repaired. Only then did she return to Britain with a cargo of meat after a voyage that lasted 14 months.

His father was silent. The rain began making wet blots on the wooden wharf.

'Dad?'

'Mine once.'

'Were you the captain?'

'Third engineer.'

His father looked at the grey hills on the far side of the harbour.

'Can we go on the ship, Dad? Can we? Dad?'

Alec looked at the ship towering above him. He watched the crane lower the empty sling back down onto the wharf. He turned and saw his father walking back to the wharf gates with his hands in his coat pockets.

'Dad, wait for me!' he yelled and ran after him.

The suitcase on top of the wardrobe

Jack's dad Alec, Wellington, 1962

'Have you got your soccer boots, Alec?' called Mary. 'Your father will take us in the car — he's out in the garage.'

Alec's father stood at the workbench in the garage with his back to them. The bonnet of the Austin was propped open. He was holding a sparkplug up to the window. The battered metal socket-set box was open on the workbench. Alec had always liked the socket set. He liked the neat row of sockets sitting in order of size and he liked the clicking sound of the ratchet when his father turned the wrench.

'I have to get the timing right,' said his father.

'Not now,' said Mary.

'I have to.'

Sandy didn't turn around to look at them.

Mary grabbed their raincoats off the back of the garage door.

'Come on, Alec,' she said. They ran out of the garage, along the concrete path beside the house and down Pirie Street to the tram stop.

Mary watched the grey clouds tumbling over the city. She looked at the dull green grass and the muddy field. She looked at her boy out on the wing. He had grown tall with long skinny legs that he didn't seem to know what to do with. His shorts flapped in the wind. His hands were tucked into his armpits to keep warm.

There was a thud as a boot connected with the ball. It came flying out of the scrappy tangle in the centre of the field. Alec kicked it on down the sideline: kick and run, kick and run, he side-stepped around his opposite number, dodged around two more defenders and booted it past the goalkeeper's gloved hands into the corner of the net.

In the second half he did it again.

Mary waited until they were walking back to the tram. 'Two-nil. They were pleased with you.' The tram came clattering up and they climbed on board. Mary noticed he could reach the leather straps hanging from the roof. She smiled at him. Alec looked out the window.

They hung their raincoats back in the garage. The bonnet of the Austin was shut. The socket-set box was shut and stowed on its shelf under the workbench.

The following Friday was Guy Fawkes night.

'Will the car be going this time?' asked Mary.

'The car is running just fine,' said Sandy.

As the sun set, they drove to the south coast.

'Hey, carry some of this,' his mum called. She collected their jackets and the basket with the tea and the sausage rolls from the boot of the car.

'Give them to me,' said his dad. 'I'll take them.'

'You okay?' she asked.

'I'll manage.'

Alec grabbed his bag of fireworks and ran down the path through the flax and the taupata. There was a fire burning on the beach. His friend Tino from the soccer team was lighting sparklers for his younger sisters who then ran around trying to write their names in the darkness.

'Sparkler?' said Tino, offering one to Alec's dad.

'No, no, not for me,' Sandy stepped back, holding his hands up.

Alec reached into his cellophane packet and pulled out a string of crackers. Tino held a match to the grey wick. Alec threw the crackers out into the darkness. There was a machine-gun clatter as the string of crackers flung itself around on the sand.

'Shit!' said his father, jumping away, hands over his head.

'Sorry,' said Alec.

Tino nailed a Catherine wheel to a driftwood log and lit the fuse — a shower of spinning sparks lit up the beach. Rockets raced skywards from soft-drink bottles. Roman candles shot showers of red, orange and purple sparks into the night. Mighty Cannons boomed.

As the bags of fireworks emptied, the pops, bangs and flashes slowed and people gathered around the fire. Alec and his mum sat down on the sand. His mother took out the tea and the cups and the sausage rolls. 'Where's your father?' she said, looking around, and then added, 'I should have brought the rug.'

'I'll get it from the car,' said Alec. He walked back up the beach, his feet crunching on the dry seaweed. He found the track back to the car and opened the door.

His father was lying on the back seat with the blanket over his head.

'Dad?'

His father sat up.

'I was just . . .'

He quickly started folding the blanket.

Alec saw his father's hands were shaking.

'I'll get Mum,' he said.

On Monday his father wasn't at the table for breakfast. His mother was silent. Alec decided it was best not to ask. On Tuesday he wasn't there either.

'He took the tram,' said his mother.

'Is he coming back?' asked Alec.

His mother looked out the window at Pirie Street. She picked his coat off the back of the chair. 'It's time for school,' she said.

'I shouldn't have set off those fireworks.'

His mother gave him a hug. 'It wasn't those fireworks.'

He learnt how to peel potatoes and set the table. On Saturdays, in summer, he would mow the back lawn with the push mower. When his father mowed the lawns, the mower had made a pleasing clicking sound and the neatly clipped grass would shoot into the canvas catcher. Now the blades clattered around munching and tearing at the grass. He looked through his father's tools in the garage wondering how to adjust the blades. The files, crescent spanners and screwdrivers hanging on the shadow board above the workbench had a brown dusting of rust.

By the end of summer, the neat rows of peas, broad beans and lettuces in his father's vegetable garden had become a tangle of long grass, onion weed and fennel stalks.

He got a job after school selling the *Evening Post* outside the railway station. He didn't have time for soccer practice.

On top of the wardrobe was his father's brown leather suitcase. One Saturday afternoon when his mother was playing golf, Alec lifted the suitcase down and laid it on the bed. Inside was a Kodak camera. He opened it — the bellows unfolded like a concertina. Under the camera was an album full of pictures of ships and ports and sailors. The first picture in the album was of a ship called the *Accra*. Its name was neatly written in white pencil on the black paper. There were pictures of crewmembers. Mr O'Malley and Mr Cooper looking flash in their uniforms, and a picture of the plumber, in overalls and a tropical helmet, asleep on deck.

Underneath the album he found a dark blue book that looked like a passport. It had the words Continuous Certificate of Discharge embossed in silver on the cover. It was a list of all the ships his father had sailed on. It began in June 1935 when he left Liverpool on the *Accra* for the west coast of Africa as the seventh engineer and ended when he was the chief engineer in March 1946. He read through the list of ships. After the *Accra* came the *Henry Stanley*, then the *Taranaki*, the *Karamea*, the *Pakeha* and the *Mahia*, all sailing out of the Victoria Docks to New Zealand. In July 1941 there was a ship called the *Sydney Star.*

Next to it, where the details of the voyage should have been, were the words 'To be completed later', written in pencil.

He remembered going down to the wharf with his father when he was six to see the *Sydney Star.* He remembered how his father stopped before he got close to the ship and then hurried away and how he was silent in the tram on the way home.

He heard his mother drive the Austin up the side of the house into the garage and come in through the back door. As she slung her golf bag behind the bedroom door, she smiled at him. 'I thought you might want to look through that one day.'

'He'd know how to sharpen the mower,' said Alec.

'He knew how to keep machines going,' agreed his mother.

'I remember starting on a holiday once,' said Alec.

'You were five,' said his mother. 'I'd persuaded him to take three days off so we could go to Napier. He was working at Luke Brothers Engineering Works in Cable Street. I thought he could take you to Marineland and I could play some golf. We got to Palmerston North and he phoned Lukes from a phone box in the Square to see how the job was going and he decided we had to go back so he could make sure it was done correctly.'

'Where is he now?' asked Alec.

'He doesn't keep in touch.'

Alec looked at the discharge book.

'Did he tell you about the ships?'

'We didn't talk about any of that.'

'What happened with the *Sydney Star*?'

His mother looked out the window. A tram clattered down Pirie Street towards the city.

'I never asked.'

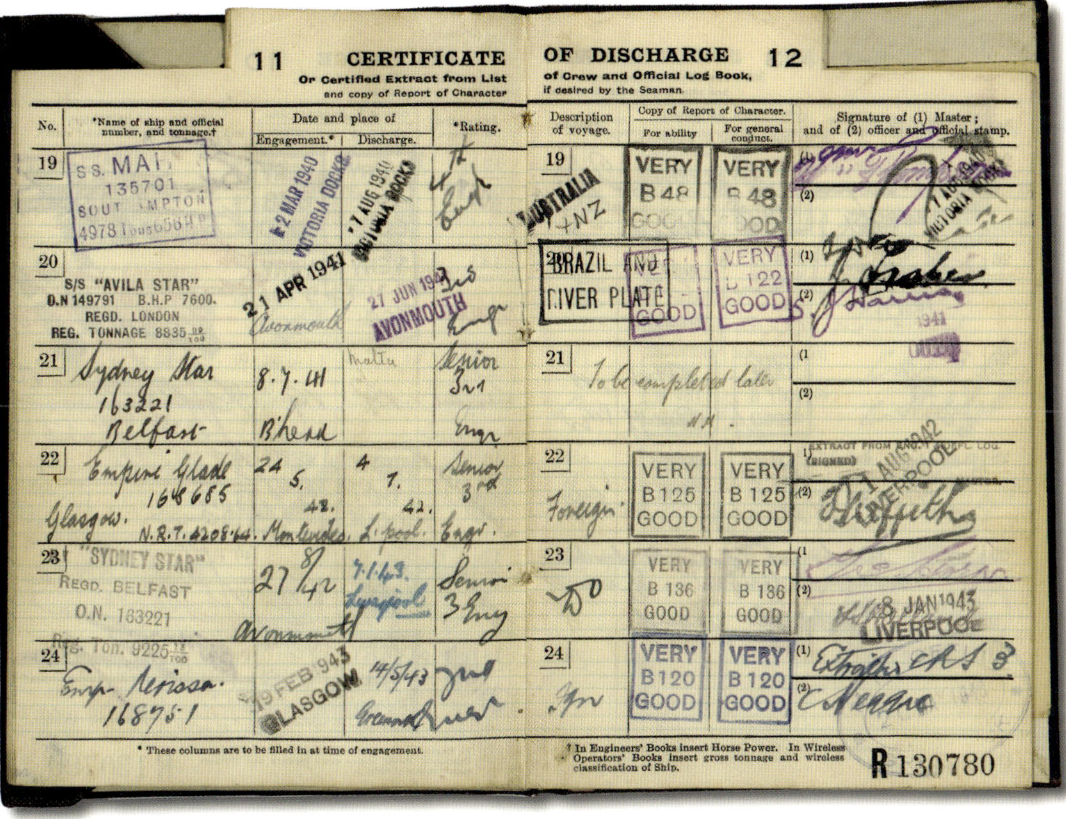

11 **CERTIFICATE** OF DISCHARGE 12

Or Certified Extract from List of Crew and Official Log Book, and copy of Report of Character if desired by the Seaman.

No.	*Name of ship and official number, and tonnage.†	Date and place of Engagement.*	Date and place of Discharge.	*Rating.	No.	Description of voyage.	Copy of Report of Character. For ability	Copy of Report of Character. For general conduct.	Signature of (1) Master; and of (2) officer and official stamp.
19	S.S. MAI[illegible] 135701 SOUTHAMPTON 4978 Tons 656 H.P.	2 MAR 1940 VICTORIA DOCKS	7 AUG 1940 VICTORIA DOCKS	4th Engr	19	AUSTRALIA + NZ	VERY B 48 GOOD	VERY B 48 GOOD	(1) [illegible] (2) 7 AUG 1940 VICTORIA DOCKS
20	S/S "AVILA STAR" O.N 149791 B.H.P 7600. REGD. LONDON REG. TONNAGE 8835 $\frac{09}{100}$	21 APR 1941 Avonmouth	27 JUN 1941 AVONMOUTH	3rd Engr	20	BRAZIL AND RIVER PLATE	VERY B 122 GOOD	VERY B 122 GOOD	(1) [illegible] (2) [illegible] 1941
21	Sydney Star 163221 Belfast	8.7.41 B'head	Malta	Senior 3rd Engr	21	To be completed later			(1) (2)
22	Empire Glade 168685 Glasgow. N.R.T. 4208·64	24.5.42. Montevideo	4.7.42. L'pool	Senior 3rd Engr.	22	Foreign	VERY B 125 GOOD	VERY B 125 GOOD	(1) EXTRACT FROM ENG. [illegible] LOG (SIGNED) (2) 7 AUG 1942 LIVERPOOL [illegible]
23	"SYDNEY STAR" REGD. BELFAST O.N. 163221 Reg. Ton. 9225 $\frac{18}{100}$	27/8/42 Avonmouth	7.1.43. Liverpool	Senior 3 Eng	23	Do	VERY B 136 GOOD	VERY B 136 GOOD	(1) [illegible] (2) 8 JAN 1943 LIVERPOOL
24	Emp. Merissa. 168751	19 FEB 1943 GLASGOW	14/5/43 Greenock	2nd Engr	24	Fgn	VERY B 120 GOOD	VERY B 120 GOOD	(1) Extract [illegible] (2) [illegible]

* These columns are to be filled in at time of engagement.

† In Engineers' Books insert Horse Power. In Wireless Operators' Books insert gross tonnage and wireless classification of Ship.

R 130780

Down the river and around the coast

Jack and Eddie, the Waihou River, 2001

Jack and Eddie were woken by the whine of a quad bike pulling into the barn.

The driver jumped off and reached up to grab a hay bale. Jack sat up in his sleeping bag, grabbed the twine around a bale and handed it down. Without saying anything, the farmer took the bale and slung it on the tray of the quad bike then turned back and said, 'Morning gentlemen.'

Eddie propped himself up on one elbow and grinned.

'Saw your kayaks tied to the fence, thought I might find somebody here.'

'Hope you don't mind,' said Jack.

'Bit late if I do,' said the farmer. 'How far do you two plan to go?'

'Auckland,' said Jack.

The farmer folded his arms and looked at them. 'Do you now?'

'That's the plan,' said Eddie.

'So you know what the weather is for the next week?'

'We knew it was going to rain yesterday,' said Jack.

'Yesterday's weather isn't much help today,' said the farmer. 'And the tides?' He added, 'Do you want to sit out there on the mudflats for hours while you wait for the tide to come back in?' He flung a fence strainer and coils of wire on top of the hay bale then sat back on the bike seat and looked at them.

'Don't drink the river water,' he said. 'There's a tap on the end of the shed. Fill your water bottles up there. You should be okay if you get across to the shell bank at Miranda on the high tide. You'll have about two hours on either side.'

The quad bike's motor whined into life. As he left, the farmer shouted over his shoulder, 'For Christ's sake tell the cops or the harbour master or somebody in Thames what your plans are.'

'Right,' said Jack to the back of the quad bike as it roared away across the paddock.

Eddie and Jack sat in the sun at the picnic table at the Cook Memorial eating muesli.

'I wonder what he had for breakfast?'

'Who?'

'Your grandad.'

'Not muesli. Porridge, I reckon,' said Jack. They packed their gear and slid the kayaks back down to the water. The outgoing tide carried them down the river. It was wide now with mangroves on either side. There was no wind. At Turua there was another concrete boat ramp next to a wharf. Jack and Eddie pulled in. One street back from the river they found the Turua Dairy and Takeaways. Eddie bought burgers. Jack bought a copy of the *Herald* and turned to the weather report and the tide tables. 'Fine tomorrow with a high tide at two-thirty. We'll have to spend tonight in Thames.'

They paddled on under the Kopu Bridge. Ahead was their first view of the open sea. They skirted around the mudflats and paddled into the Kauaeranga River to the wharf.

'Pull up there,' called a man painting the cabin of a motorboat. He waved his paintbrush at a slimy boat ramp at the end of the wharf.

'Where have you guys come from?' he asked when they had pulled up their kayaks.

'Stanley Landing,' said Jack.

'Is there somewhere here we could camp?' asked Eddie.

'Not here,' said the painter and carried on painting white trim around the door to the cabin. Jack and Eddie pulled their bags and the tent out and looked around.

'I could go a burger,' said Eddie.

The painter poured turpentine from a bottle into a tin can, sloshed his brush around in it and wiped it dry, and looked at the two of them.

'At the back of the car plant,' he said, waving the paintbrush at a large warehouse behind the boats.

'Eh?' said Eddie.

'There's a patch of grass between the car plant and the mangroves. Put your tent up there — nobody should bother you.'

TOWARDS THE SHELL BANK AT MIRANDA.

WHAT DO YOU KNOW ABOUT FISHING, JACK?
NOT MUCH, JUST TOW IT ALONG BEHIND AND SEE WHAT HAPPENS.

IT'S A FISH. WHAT DO I DO NOW?

STUFF IT UNDER YOUR SPRAY-SKIRT.
THERE'S GOT TO BE A BETTER SYSTEM.

LATER THAT AFTERNOON.
CAPTAIN, SIR, WE APPEAR TO BE RUNNING OUT OF SEA.

NICE ONE.
THE FISHBURGER.
THE SUNSET?

The next morning when the tide came back in, they set off. As they paddled north, a wind came up.

'It's like a slow-motion rollercoaster,' shouted Eddie as he rose up and down on the big swells. Jack kept his eye on the waves breaking as they rolled into the beach. 'We should be okay if we stay out a bit,' he shouted to Eddie. They paddled around Ōrere Point. The wind and the swells grew. 'I reckon we should head for the beach in the lee of those rocks,' he yelled. Eddie stopped paddling and turned to look over his shoulder. 'What did you say?' he called. As he lost forward momentum the wind blew his kayak side on to the lumpy swell, then a sudden gust flipped it right over. Eddie bobbed up, wide-eyed, beside the upside-down kayak. 'Shit, how did that happen?'

Jack grabbed the bow of Eddie's kayak. Eddie reached over his upturned boat and grabbed the deck lines on the far side. Jack lifted the bow out of the water. Eddie heaved. The kayak felt like it was full of concrete. 'Try again!' Jack yanked the bow up. Eddie heaved. The kayak flopped over. The cockpit was awash. Eddie had one arm over his waterlogged kayak. With the other he held onto the back of Jack's boat. He kicked; Jack paddled. It felt like they were towing a wallowing hippopotamus. After five long minutes, they were in the shelter of the rocks. After a few more minutes, Eddie felt sand beneath his feet. He let the kayak go. A wave tumbled it into the beach. Jack surfed the next wave in.

They dragged the kayaks up the beach, past the line of driftwood and dry seaweed at the high-water mark.

Eddie was shaking. 'Come on, get on some dry clothes.' Jack grabbed the dry bags out of the back hatch. He found a sheltered hollow in the dunes and fished around in the food bag. He found a packet of pumpkin soup and the gas stove. It was only when he had the pumpkin soup simmering that he realised he was freezing as well.

'You should have seen your face as you tipped,' he said, passing Eddie a steaming mug.

Later in the afternoon, warm in their jeans, jackets and woolly hats, they walked down the coast, bending under the gnarly branches of pōhutukawa trees leaning out from the cliffs.

'Let's try up there,' said Eddie, pointing up a gully. They climbed through knee-high kikuyu grass and pūriri trees to the cliff top and looked down at the sea. The wind had fallen away.

'Hard to imagine now how we got into trouble out there,' said Jack as they walked back along the cliff tops.

'Did your mysterious grandad ever get into trouble?' asked Eddie. 'Was he bombed, machine-gunned, sunk, did he end up in the sea?

'I don't know,' said Jack. 'I asked Gran once, before she went gaga, and all she said was "He couldn't swim — he was scared of the water".'

'Jeez,' muttered Eddie, feeling again the gust that flipped his kayak and the shock of the water.

'It's too late now,' went on Jack, 'she just smiles and asks me who I am, and I tell her "I'm your grandson," and she says, "Are you really?" and then she'll ask me, "Why didn't he bail out?" and I'll say "Who?" and she'll say, "I don't know."'

'Weird,' said Eddie.

Back at the kayaks, Jack looked at Eddie. 'Okay?'

Eddie nodded. They paddled for two more hours up the coast on a flat, calm sea. When the sun disappeared behind the inland hills, they started looking for a place to camp.

The next day they started at dawn. When the wind sprang up in the middle of the morning, they pulled into the shelter of the next promontory, climbed the hill and looked out over the islands. The wind rippled the long grass in the paddocks and whipped up whitecaps out in the gulf. When the wind fell away in the late afternoon, they paddled across to Whakakaiwhara and camped for the night.

On the sixth day there was no midday wind. After a week of paddling, Jack could feel the power in his arms. He had a big bottle of water under the bungee cords and five muesli bars stuffed into his lifejacket. He felt he could paddle forever. On they went, hour after hour, through the long afternoon away out in the middle of the channel. The empty beaches began to fill with holiday houses and then the holiday houses turned into the Auckland suburbs of Maraetai and Beachlands. In early evening, off Howick, they rafted up, unfolded their map and spread it across the spray-skirts.

'Where are we going to pitch up for the night?' said Eddie. 'It's all houses now.'

'There are no houses here,' said Jack, pointing at a long peninsula snaking out towards Rangitoto Island. 'We could try there.' They paddled on. The sky turned from blue to pink, and then the pink turned to orange and then the orange faded to grey.

'We should have a light,' said Jack. 'No one can see us out here.'

'Any more muesli bars?' asked Eddie. Jack shook his head.

They paddled on in the dark. Just before they came to the point of the peninsula, they saw a gap in the rocks that led to a small beach backed by sandstone cliffs. They pulled the kayaks up the sand under the pōhutukawa trees. Jack took the top off the back hatch and fumbled around until he found his torch.

The sun shining in under the pōhutukawa trees woke them early. They hadn't bothered with the tent. They had just unrolled their sleeping bags on the warm sand and slept. On their gas stove Jack made tea and a large billy of porridge. They packed up and pushed off and paddled around the point. There, rising out of the mist in the distance, were the tall buildings of the city catching the early-morning light. To their left were beaches with cafés and ice-cream parlours. On the headlands between the beaches were huge houses surrounded by palm trees. Joggers pounded along Tamaki Drive. In the distance a stream of cars crawled over the Harbour Bridge like ants on a coat hanger. In front of the bridge, blunt-nosed ferries dashed back and forth across the harbour from Devonport.

'That's where we're headed,' said Jack. 'The ferry terminal at the bottom of Queen Street.'

'Will there be somewhere we can land?' said Eddie.

'Bound to be,' said Jack. 'There'll be steps or something.'

In the middle of the morning a south-westerly breeze sprang up. They could see the museum on its hill in the middle of the Domain and the square grey hospital building on the ridge top. Ahead of them was the container terminal with stacks of red, grey and blue containers and a row of cranes like giant stick insects. They bounced over the wake of two tugs that were heading down the harbour. The seaman in the wheelhouse gave them a wave. A silver keeler motored past. The people in the cockpit were all wearing the same crisp white T-shirts. Eddie waved. They didn't wave back.

Late in the morning they passed the end of Queens Wharf and turned towards the red-brick ferry building. There was a loud blast on a horn behind them. A huge ferry was also pulling in. It gave a second thundering blast on its horn. Their plastic kayaks crunched on the mussel-encrusted piles as they backpaddled under the wharf. A green glow of reflected light played on the roof above them. Black wharf piles disappeared in neat rows into the darkness. They edged the kayaks around and peered back out into the sunlight. Ferries kept coming and going, dropping their passengers, collecting more and then churning the water up as they backed out and turned around.

'Plan B?' enquired Eddie as he jammed his paddle against a pile to steady himself.

'Somewhere else,' suggested Jack. They waited for a gap and paddled frantically from under the wharf back out into the harbour. Their kayaks slapped up and down through the south-westerly swell. In the middle of the harbour Jack could see whitecaps. Past the tank farm they came to Westhaven Marina — acres of aluminium masts bobbing back and forth like a field of metronomes, the rigging clattering against them in the wind.

'Let's try in there,' called Eddie.

Behind the rows of yachts and motorboats they saw a small beach with a neatly mown lawn behind it. They stopped paddling ten metres out from the beach and sat there looking at the lawn.

'We're here then,' said Jack.

'Yep, we're here,' said Eddie. With a few more paddle strokes the kayaks crunched into the sand. They stepped out and hauled the kayaks out of the water. Eddie looked at his watch. 'It's one-thirty. Time to go and find your grandad.'

The bus to the Ranfurly Veterans Home made its way up Symonds Street past the university engineering school.

'That could be you next year,' said Eddie, pointing out the window at students with backpacks hurrying to their next lecture.

'According to Dad,' said Jack.

He was looking further up Symonds Street at the road that went down the hill to the art school . . .

'I've come to see Mr Tait,' said Jack.

'Sandy Tait,' said the receptionist. 'You're his . . . ?'

'Grandson.'

'You phoned, didn't you?'

Jack nodded.

'I'll go and ask.'

Eddie sat down in an armchair in the waiting room. Jack waited by the counter. Five minutes later the receptionist came back.

'Mr Tait won't see you. I'm sorry.'

'He can't.'

'He doesn't know anything about a grandson.'

'Well, he could find out. I've spent a week with a wet arse in a kayak and nearly drowned myself and he can't be bothered. What room is he in?'

'I can't tell you that,' said the receptionist.

Jack turned and walked back to the waiting room and slumped down in a chair next to Eddie.

'So what now?'

'Don't know.'

'Selfish old bastard.'

They sat in silence.

Eddie picked a magazine from the top of the pile beside his chair. A woman in a blue smock started mopping the tiled floor at the front entrance. When she finished, she set up a yellow plastic sign that read Caution, Wet Floor. Eddie flicked through his magazine — *Purnell's History of the Second World War.* 'The General Who Never Lost a Battle,' he read out aloud, 'General Zhukov tells how he planned the Moscow counterblow.'

'That's what we need,' said Jack, 'a counterblow.'

The woman in the blue smock left with her bucket and mop and came back ten minutes later pushing a tea trolley.

'I could go a cup of tea,' said Eddie. 'If I grab the attention of the receptionist, you could nick off down the corridor and find your grandad. I'll see you at my auntie's place in Gillies Avenue. You can walk there from here.'

'Let's give it a shot,' said Jack.

Eddie scooped the bundle of *Purnell's History of the Second World War* off the table and headed towards the reception desk, tripped over the yellow sign, flung the magazines in the air and hit the floor with a thump. The receptionist rushed out from behind the front desk. 'Are you okay?'

While she was helping Eddie up, Jack ducked off down the corridor. 'That floor really was slippery,' he heard Eddie say.

The corridor was lined with numbered doors. The carpet was orange and brown and well worn. He reached an intersection. Left or right? he wondered. The woman with the tea trolley came clattering past.

'Sandy Tait?' asked Jack.

'Room 27, love,' she said, pointing left. 'Tell him I'll be along soon with his cuppa.'

Jack knocked on the door of room 27.

Jack waited. His grandfather turned around.

'Who the hell are you?'

'I'm Jack.'

'I don't do visitors.'

'I'm not a visitor, I'm your grandson.'

His grandfather folded his arms and looked at him in silence.

'I'm leaving the mobility scooter to the home. That's all there is.'

This wasn't how Jack had imagined the conversation starting. He took his parka off and sat down in a plastic chair by the door.

'I didn't invite you to stay.'

'I haven't come for your bloody mobility scooter. I came here to meet you before you . . . I just thought . . .'

'Best not to think,' said his grandfather. 'How did you get past the front desk?'

'Took General Zhukov's advice,' he said, 'and struck a counterblow.'

His grandfather stared at him. Jack could see this wasn't going to go anywhere. He stood up and turned towards the door.

'Good chap,' said his grandfather.

'Well, thanks,' said Jack.

'Not you, General Zhukov. It was the Russians who won the war; we were just a sideshow.'

Jack sat down again.

'How did you find me?'

'Dad tried to keep track of you by going through the electoral rolls in the library,' said Jack.

'Did he ever say anything against me?'

'Well, he didn't say it to you because you weren't there. All he had was your photograph album.'

His grandfather looked up, surprised, and then asked, 'And Mary, is she . . . ?'

'Gran lives with us. She still plays golf, but she's missing in action now. I carry her golf clubs — she doesn't really know who I am, but we have a good time. She remembers some things, but it's all jumbled. She keeps asking me, "When is Aunt Adina coming?"'

There was another long silence.

'How did you get here?'

Jack laughed. 'By boat.'

'You sailed?'

'We paddled — me and my mate Eddie. We came ashore at Westhaven, by the Harbour Bridge, locked the kayaks to the fence with my bicycle lock and caught the bus here.'

'Where did you start?'

'At Stanley Landing.'

His grandfather stood up and looked through a row of books on a wooden shelf above the bed. He pulled out an old school atlas with a red and black cover. 'Where's this Stanley Landing?' Jack found the page with a map of the North Island. He traced his finger down the Waihou River, around the Firth of Thames and into the Waitematā Harbour.

'You paddled all that way,' said his grandfather, looking at him closely for the first time. 'Any mishaps?'

'A couple.'

'I did a few sea journeys myself.'

'I know,' said Jack. He reached into his parka pocket, took out the discharge book and laid it on the end of the bed.

'Jeezus!' His grandfather snatched it up. 'I haven't seen this since 1946.' He opened it and slowly turned each page. 'Ah, the *Karamea*, that was a happy ship.'

The tea trolley clattered to a halt at the door.

'Two sugars for me, Netta, and a cup of tea for the boy — he's my grandson, he's come to visit me.'

'You're not supposed to have sugar, Mr Tait.'

'It doesn't matter what I have now, and give the boy some of those chocolate biscuits.'

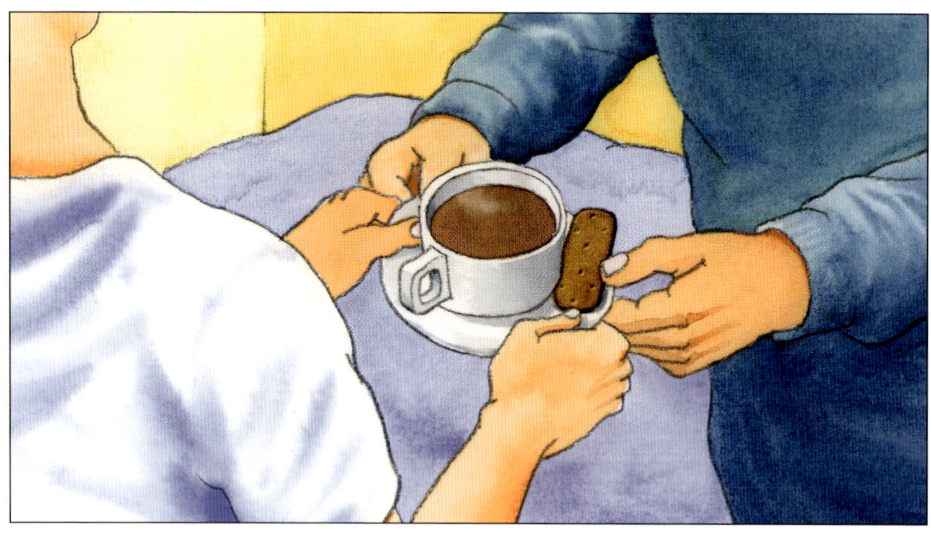

Jack took a cup of tea and handed it to his grandfather.

'The girl makes a good cup of tea,' his grandfather said without looking up.

'I'm sixty-two, Mister Tait. I retire next year,' said Netta. She thrust the packet of Chocolate Thins at Jack. 'Take a handful, love. He's a pussycat really,' and then she trundled the trolley off to the next room.

'There are no details for the *Sydney Star*,' said Jack.

'Blue Star Line. It was new and fast. Mind you, it needed to be.'

'Where was it going?' asked Jack.

'We sailed out of Liverpool, but nobody knew. By the time we were halfway across the Bay of Biscay we could guess.'

'We?' said Jack.

'Me and my mate Billy. He was the sparks, and I was the third engineer.'

Once his grandfather started talking, he couldn't stop. It all poured out. The great armada of ships that had been assembled to protect them, sailing through the Straits of Gibraltar at midnight in the fog. The first two days of their mad dash to Malta when they thought they might get away with it, the circling spotter plane. The first bomber attack that destroyed the *Fearless* and sent the *Manchester* limping back to Gibraltar. The fight with the torpedo boats off Pantelleria, the torpedo slamming into the *Sydney Star*. Their desperate battle to keep the ship afloat and their entry into the Grand Harbour with the bands playing.

'After the ship was unloaded, we had a chance to look around. I thought things were bad in Liverpool, but Malta was worse.'

HAIR CUTTING
SALOON

. . . BILLY HAD GONE DEAF FROM THE GUNFIRE.
BAR
TRIQ ID-DEJQA
STRAIT STREET

BAR

WHAT WERE YOU ON?
THE *FEARLESS*.
IT WAS THE BLOKES AFT THAT COPPED IT.

CROSBY?

AFT.

BAR
LET'S GET OUT OF TOWN.

BUS STATION

BUS
RABAT
MEDINA
RABAT

RABAT

CHRIST!
IT WAS SAFER IN BOMB ALLEY.

THE AIRFIELD'S GETTING IT.

NOW, THERE'S A PICTURE.

IF WE ARE GOING TO CATCH THE LAST BUS BACK...
YOU GO, I'LL CATCH UP.

BILLY!

'Billy didn't hear me shouting.

'He didn't hear the fighter.

'He didn't hear the burst of cannon fire.'

Jack's grandfather stopped talking and sat for a long time in silence.

Jack waited.

'Nothing was the same after that. Everyone I was close to . . .' his grandfather's voice trailed off. 'Yes, we patched up the ship and made a dash for Alexandria and again we were bombed and again they missed, and we sailed through the Suez Canal and across the Atlantic to Buenos Aires where it took three months to repair the ship's refrigeration equipment and replace the patch over the hole. I didn't get Billy home.'

'So you left.'

'We all leave home.'

'And then you left Dad.'

'He was okay.'

'No, he wasn't.'

'He was a young man.'

'He was fourteen.'

'Look, I did the best I could.'

'So just say that to Dad.'

'That's all in the past now. I've talked too much.'

'You haven't talked enough. You went missing.'

Jack looked out the window at the sun setting over the city. A few streets away Eddie would be sitting in his aunt's kitchen telling her about camping in the hay barn.

'How did you get to Stanley Landing?' asked his grandfather.

'Dad dropped us off.'

'Looks after you, does he?'

'A bit too much sometimes. He worries, wants to make sure I make the right decision so he makes all the decisions for me. Next year I'll be finishing school, leaving home.'

'To do what?'

'I'm supposed to enrol for an engineering degree.'

'Supposed to?'

'That's what Dad wants me to do. He says we've always been engineers.'

'Billy and me — we didn't have a choice,' said his grandfather. 'There was no university for the likes of us. It was the shipyard or the ship. I was planning to swallow the anchor when I got back from Townsville in 1939. I got to the end of the wharf and a chap in a tin hut at the gate said,

"There's a war on, lad. When your leave's over you report to the ship."

'See here,' he opened the discharge book and read out the last entry: '"Released on termination of war service — May 1946." I had to put in another six years sailing around being shot at. I was thirty-two years old when I got my life back. You can choose. What is it that you want to do?'

Jack paused. 'Dad says I can't earn a living at it, but . . .'

'I didn't ask what your dad wants, I asked what you want.'

'Art school.'

His grandfather held up his hand. He stood up and went back to the bookcase and looked through the books one by one.

'Here it is.' He pulled out a sketchbook and handed it to Jack.

Jack turned the pages. They were filled with pencil drawings of passenger liners and merchant ships. The second to last drawing was of a ship with the words '*Sydney Star,* July 1941' written underneath. The last drawing was of a small stone building on a cliff top.

'That was Billy's sketch book. You keep it now. You do what Billy could never do. You go to art school.'

'I'd be in the city — a bus ride away,' he said. 'I could bring your photograph album and you could tell me about the ships.'

For the first time Jack saw his grandfather smile. 'Yeah, I could tell you a thing or two about the ships.'

'At the start of the term Dad will help me move my stuff. Perhaps we could both come.'

There was a long awkward silence. His grandfather turned away and looked out the window, shaking his head.

The trees outside were dark against the fading light.

His grandfather sighed and turned back to face him.

'I guess it's never . . .' then he stopped.

Jack waited.

'I guess there's still . . .'

Jack waited.

'. . . still time. Yes, bring your dad.'

His grandfather held out his hand. 'You head off now — your mate Eddie will be wondering where you are.'

Operation Substance

On 10 June 1940 the Italian fascist leader Benito Mussolini stood on the balcony of the Palazzo Venezia in Rome and announced to the crowd in the square below that Italy had joined Adolf Hitler and declared war on Britain and France.

The following morning the citizens of Malta woke to the sound of air-raid sirens and exploding bombs. It was the beginning of a bombing campaign and blockade intended to force the island to surrender. Malta had to be supplied by convoys from Gibraltar in the west and Egypt in the east. The siege ended in November 1942.

Malta finally gained its independence from Britain in 1964.

On 12 July 1941 Operation Substance, a convoy of six merchant ships loaded with food, men, medicine and arms, sailed from Liverpool for Gibraltar and Malta. This convoy was protected by twenty-five navy ships.

The *Sydney Star* was the largest merchant ship in the convoy. It was a fast modern cargo ship from the Blue Star Line. On board were a regiment of troops and a cargo of food, fuel, medical supplies, aircraft engines, anti-aircraft guns and ammunition.

Thomas Horn was the Captain of the *Sydney Star*. He first went to sea when he was fifteen. He worked his way up through the ranks and became a ship's master in 1924.

The *Fearless* was one of the destroyers protecting the merchant ships. It was hit by a torpedo during the first attack on 23 July. Thirty-seven of the crew of the *Fearless* were killed.

The *Nestor* was the Australian Navy destroyer that found the *Sydney Star* after it had been torpedoed near the island of Pantelleria. The *Nestor* was joined by the cruiser *Hermione*. They fought off three more attacks as they shepherded the damaged *Sydney Star* on its final dash to Malta.

Robert Kerr, the author's father, was the inspiration for the fictional story of Jack and Sandy. He was born in Greenock, Scotland, in 1913 and went to sea on the *Accra* in 1935. In 1941 he was the third engineer on the *Sydney Star*. With Chief Engineer Frank Haig, Chief Officer Mr Machie, the ship's carpenter Frank Bones and other crewmembers he succeeded in getting the damaged ship to Valletta's Grand Harbour. Photographs he took during his time at sea have been used to illustrate *Jack & Sandy*.

On 20 July 1941, the ships of Operation Substance sail through the Straits of Gibraltar hidden by thick fog. On the morning of the 22nd, an Italian spotter plane finds the convoy.

On the morning of 23 July, Italian torpedo bombers flying from Sardinia attack the convoy. The cruiser *Manchester* is hit and the destroyer *Fearless* is sunk.

On the evening of 23 July, the aircraft carrier *Ark Royal* and the big warships turn back. It is too dangerous for them to sail through the Skerki Channel between Sicily and Tunisia.

During the night of 23 July the convoy sails through the minefield north of the island of Pantelleria. At three in the morning they run into a patrol of Italian torpedo boats. The *Sydney Star* is hit by a torpedo.

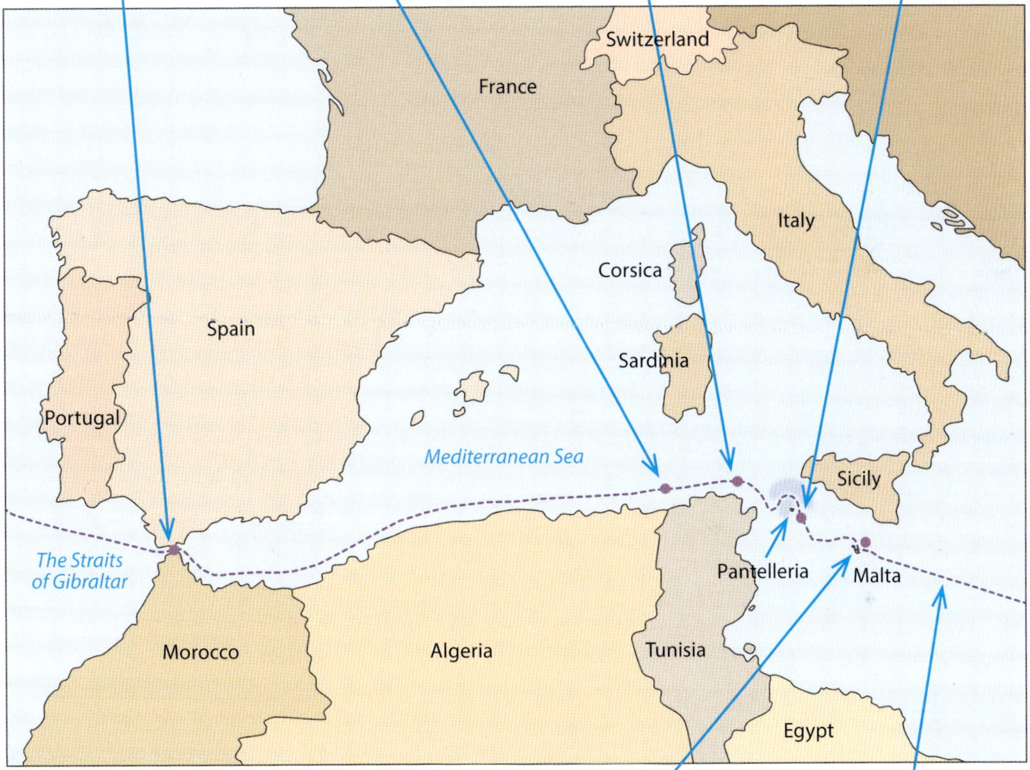

Switzerland
France
Italy
Corsica
Spain
Sardinia
Portugal
Mediterranean Sea
Sicily
The Straits of Gibraltar
Pantelleria
Malta
Morocco
Algeria
Tunisia
Egypt

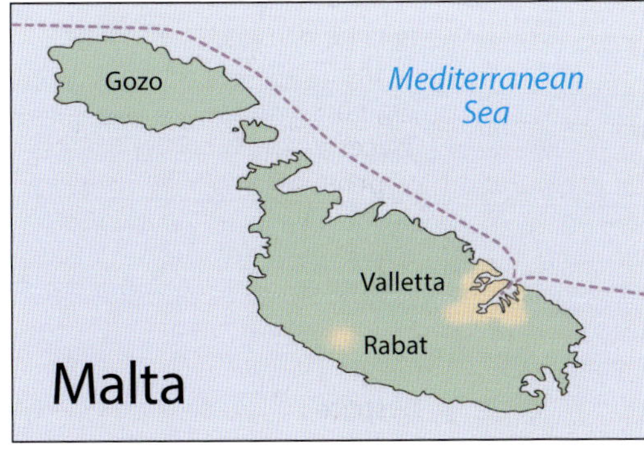

On the afternoon of 24 July, the *Sydney Star* sails into Malta's Grand Harbour. All the merchant ships of Operation Substance and their valuable cargoes arrive safely.

On 26 December, the patched-up *Sydney Star* sails from Malta to Alexandria in Egypt. It is attacked again, but the bombs and torpedoes miss, and it arrives on 29 December.

Published in 2023 by David Bateman Ltd
2/5 Workspace Drive
Hobsonville, Auckland 0618
New Zealand

www.batemanbooks.co.nz

ISBN 978-1-77689-063-7

Illustrations by: Bob Kerr

Photographs: Robert Kerr

Book design: Bob Kerr and minimum graphics

Printed in China by Asia Pacific Offset